THE LONG CON (STANDARD EDITION)

The Long Con (Standard Edition)

JI Y. SON

Informed
Consent
Press

Author's Note

This story was inspired by something real: an extraordinary love story, offhandedly recounted to me by a skeptical storyteller. Neither of us believed it at first. Not really. Not until we were texted a photo. Two people had built something through letters that, improbably and unimaginably, lasted through time, distance, and the American legal system.

I don't know them. I've never met them. This is not their story. The characters here are entirely fictional. The letters, the details, the emotional arc, the voice–it's all imagined.

But the inspiration was real.

And if this manuscript ever finds its way to the two people who sparked it, I hope they won't be offended by everything I made up. This is not a biography. It's not even close.

It's a kind of tribute. A "thank you" to a story that seemed too impossible to be true... and therefore demanded *fiction*.

–JYS

Part 1

Seoul

Present Day

She holds up a pair of ridiculous sushi earrings next to her ear and peeks sideways into the mirror. Tuna–magenta and white, gleaming under the too-bright lights like tiny jokes. Long, lean legs in jean shorts. Striped socks. Birkenstock-style slippers. Her silky black hair falls into place even when she laughs. And that slouch–awkward but endearing, unpolished but full of charm. Effortless and loose in the way only sixteen can be. She's not trying to be anything. Just... alive.

The kind of beautiful that doesn't know it yet. The kind that only exists in Dongdaemun Market, looking for earrings for her best friend, who somehow shares her taste in food, fashion, and birthdates.

She turns and flashes them at me, presses them to her ears and bats her eyes. I scrunch up my nose in a cringe. She grins. Then in perfect Korean, with the perfect amount of politeness called for in the moment: ("Excuse me, do you happen to have salmon earrings too?")

Fluent. Flawless. No hesitation.

The shopkeeper disappears behind a stack of plastic trays to look.

She turns her attention to the next rack: fried egg and bacon earrings. A K-pop song plays overhead, all glitter and breathy vowels. She bops along without thinking.

I watch her move through it all like she belongs here. Like she always has.

My accent is still terrible after all these years. I still flatten my vowels. Still stumble over the syllables I should've learned a long time ago. I use formal speech when I'm supposed to be casual and casual phrases when I should be showing respect.

But through her, I see what it looks like to glide. To move through the world with the silent knowledge of rightness, of knowing how to do everything without pausing to ask. Just the right words. With the right inflection. At the right time. Everything she says, and everything she doesn't, just sounds right.

She turns back to me, eyes bright, earrings swinging. "I want to get these *geeguri* for Sunah's *sengil!*"

She doesn't even pause. Just flips the words back and forth like both languages were made to sit in her mouth at once. It's not English. Not Korean. Not even a mash-up. It's fluent. It's hers.

And I nod. Because of course.

Los Angeles/
Lompoc - 2011

1.

Dear Mr. Shin,

Hi, I'm Jessica Cooper. I guess I'm writing because my best friend and I both signed up for this correspondence project through one of my classes at UCLA. We were told we'd be paired with someone who's incarcerated and that we could write about... well, anything really. No pressure, right?

I don't really know what I'm supposed to say in a first letter to a total stranger. I've never done this before. I imagine you get that a lot.

All I know is your name, Juwon Shin, and that you're currently at FCI Lompoc. I guess you also only know my name and my institution (although I guess it's a little weird to compare UCLA to a federal prison). And if you knew my full name (Jessica Minjee Cooper), you'd also know that I'm Korean too. Kind of. Sort of. Technically. (It's complicated.)

Anyway, I guess I just wanted to say hi. No expectations here. If you don't feel like writing back, that's totally fine. I wouldn't blame you. But if you do feel like writing back, I'd appreciate it.

Sincerely,
Jessica

The unit was loud again. Someone had been mouthing off to a CO and now everyone was paying for it–no dayroom, no rec, no TV. Just the sound of dominoes slapping plastic tabletops and some guy beatboxing into a cup like it was a mic.

James Juwon Shin sat on his bunk, shirtless, his back against the cinderblock wall, reading the letter.

The paper felt thin in his hands. Fancy, too. Cream-colored, with smooth corners. Folded neat. A whiff of something faintly floral. Lotion maybe. Or shampoo. Rich girl shampoo.

Jessica Minjee Cooper.

UCLA.

Of course.

He skimmed it once, then again slower. A Korean college girl (maybe adopted? maybe half?) pouring her liberal guilt into a hand-addressed envelope. She probably wore wire-rimmed glasses and Doc Martens and carried a canvas tote that said "Abolish Prisons." She'd get bored after two letters. They all did.

He wasn't even sure why he signed up for the program. Boredom, probably. Curiosity. Some guy on his block said it was a way to meet women who wanted to save a broken man. Or sleep with one. Neither turned out to be true. Mostly it was weirdos with bleeding hearts and no follow-through.

And even though he didn't expect anything, this letter seemed different from whatever he expected. Kinda blunt. Kinda funny. There was a sharpness under the politeness. She compared UCLA to FCI Lompoc. And she'd tossed off that *"Korean too. Kind of. Sort of. Technically."* line like it was a joke, but she didn't feel the need to explain. Just left it there.

He folded the letter back up, tucked it under his mattress. Then he sat for a minute, just staring at the wall. He exhaled through his nose, sharp and annoyed. At himself, mostly. He didn't have the energy to resist.

Whatever.

He'd write back.

Letters were slow. But prison was slower.

2.

Dear Jessica Minjee Cooper,
  Thanks for your letter.
  It <u>is</u> weird-writing to a complete stranger. If I were on the outside, I probably wouldn't waste my time writing to someone in prison so part of me wonders if this is a scam. A UCLA girl with a Korean middle name writing to a Korean guy in here? Feels a little... on the nose.
  Are you really a UCLA student? If so, what's your major? Why aren't you out partying with frat boys instead of writing letters to inmates?
  And you said you're kind of, sort of, technically Korean. What's that about?
  I'll be real with you–most people stop writing after two or three letters. They mean well, but life moves on. Maybe you'll write for the length of your class. No hard feelings if that's the case. But if you write again, I'll write back.
  -James Juwon Shin

She found the envelope stuck in the metal mailbox in the front lobby–the kind with too many little locked doors and a slot labeled Outgoing. She almost missed it. Most of the mail was junk: coupons, a J.Crew catalog addressed to a former tenant, a pre-approved credit card offer for "J. Cooper."
  The envelope was different. Thin, white, slightly too stiff. Her name written cleanly in the center. An equally neat re-

turn address with a blocky barcode and an official stamp on the corner: *FCI LOMPOC*. It felt like finding evidence of Santa. Or zombies. Long after she'd stopped believing.

She hadn't really expected him to write back.

It was late. The fluorescent light in the lobby flickered like a haunted hospital. Upstairs, one of her roommates was probably making boxed mac and cheese or chastising her boyfriend over speakerphone. Jessica stood still and tore the envelope open right there, next to the mailboxes.

Inside: a single sheet of lined paper, ruled in light blue, folded with military precision. It felt weirdly clean. Crisp. Bureaucratic. Like something that had been processed and passed through laser inspection before it reached her.

She unfolded it and her eyes quickly flicked down the page. He thought she might be a scam? Like... what? A catfish? A trap? The idea was so absurd it almost made her laugh. She was the least scammy person she knew. She didn't even know how to buy Bitcoin. Her Venmo was permanently locked because she lost her password one too many times and then changed her phone number. Besides, why would anyone want to scam prisoners?

She kept reading.

His tone was dry. Direct. Suspicious. He asked questions. Why wasn't she out partying with frat bros?

She smirked. As if that were the only alternative to writing to someone in prison. He was probably very old. Like a dad who worried about his college-aged daughter. Like someone who would leave voicemails and assume that they would be listened to.

And then the question about her being "*kind of, sort of, technically*" Korean. She paused there for a beat. The way he'd written it. Not mocking, exactly. Just... curious. Probing, maybe.

She felt the dull edge of the paper as she read. Somewhere upstairs, a door slammed. She was still standing in the lobby, still in her hoodie and jeans, backpack sliding off one shoulder.

Maybe she'd write back. Maybe this was more interesting than O-Chem.

3.

Dear James or Mr. Shin,

I'm not really sure what I should call you. My more Asian friends are always careful about things like that-asking elders what name to use, checking if it's respectful or too casual. I guess I never grew up with that kind of thing, so I'm still learning.

So... let's say I'm scamming you. What would I be able to steal?

Anyway, thanks for replying. I didn't think this whole letter writing thing actually worked. But for the record, I'm a real UCLA student. I almost wasn't. I was waitlisted and only got in during winter quarter of my first year, so every day I feel weirdly grateful to be one of 300 people in a lecture hall, reduced to my nine-digit student ID. In return, I get to walk the storied hallways of Royce Hall and roam a campus that's used in almost every movie as "college." And I wouldn't have met my four other roommates, who also operate as my best friends and sometimes my worst influences.

As for the "sorta" Korean thing, it's something I'm grappling with right now. UCLA has one of the highest concentrations of Asian-American students in the country. This is the campus that invented Asian-American studies as a major. But I barely feel Asian. I was adopted as a baby by white parents and lived in the outskirts of Nashville, TN for most of my life. So the only thing Korean about me is my middle name. I'm not an Asian-American studies major either. Just neuroscience.

Are you a real prisoner? Since I told you my major, will you tell me what you went to jail for?

And just to spite you, maybe I'll quit writing after four letters.

Sincerely,
Jessica

He didn't mean to read it right there.

Mail call had just ended, and the hallway was moving. Guys heading back to their units, a CO barking half-heartedly about tier rotations. Noise bounced off the concrete. But James was still, leaning with one foot against the wall, the envelope already torn open, holding the letter with both hands like it was grounding him.

Her handwriting was messy. Rushed. Loopy in places, cramped in others. She probably wrote it with her shoes kicked off, half-watching American Idol, just jotting things down between sips of something overpriced that had no pumpkin in it, but was still called pumpkin spice.

"*Mr. Shin,*" an elder. He snorted. She thought he was old. Not just older–old. Like he wore reading glasses and offered unsolicited advice to cashiers. She probably thought he sat in the prison library with a blanket warming his shoulders, reading Zen and the Art of Motorcycle Maintenance and reflecting on "the journey."

It was almost funny. She was probably, what, eighteen? Maybe nineteen? She had no idea. And he couldn't blame her. He felt old. Not in years, but in... lives. He'd lived about four since high school. Maybe five. And none of them had involved lecture halls or roommates or any of that bright-eyed, bushy-tailed campus nonsense she described.

Still.

She said she was adopted. Dropped it like it was just a line in a resume: *Korean name, neuroscience major, adopted.* No fluff. No drama. But something in the way she phrased it–"*the only Korean thing about me is my middle name*"–echoed in his mind. Not in a bad way. Just... it lingered.

He didn't want to be creepy. He knew how some guys got with these pen-pal letters: projecting things, turning strangers into girlfriends in their heads, having a lot of inappropriate thoughts. He wasn't trying to do that. This wasn't that.

Still, he found himself wondering. Was she awkward? Skinny? The kind of girl who kept her head down in class but always took the best notes? She had to be frumpy and dumpy. Definitely less than average in the looks department. A good personality kind of girl. You don't write to strangers in prison if you've got a swarm of frat boys chasing you around.

And maybe–though he'd never admit it, even to himself–he simply hoped she wasn't attractive. Not because it mattered. But because then it wouldn't matter when she stopped writing. When she got bored, or distracted, or embarrassed by this whole thing, it wouldn't smart. He was just trying to let it be what it was. Nothing. A letter. A conversation. A way to pass time.

He folded the letter slowly, since he had all the time in the world. Slipped it into his waistband and started walking.

He didn't know why, but it felt like he'd just been asked a question, and now his brain wouldn't shut up about it.

4.

Dear Jessica (Minjee? Ms. Cooper?),

I'll let you keep calling me Mr. Shin if it makes you feel better. Sounds formal as hell, but it's kind of funny coming from someone who's most stressful life event is probably midterms. My friends call me James. You choose.

Yeah, I'm a real prisoner. You're a real student. We've established our credentials.

You asked what I went to jail for. That's not really beginner-level conversation, but I get why you're curious. Let's just say I made some bad business decisions early on in life. Wrong product. Wrong logistics. Wrong side of the law. The kind of thing that lands you in federal, not state. If I'd taken a few different turns, maybe I'd be in Westwood too–getting an MBA, selling overpriced lattes instead of... other things.

I've got time to think about it now. A lot of time.

You said you were adopted, that you barely feel Korean. What do you mean by "feel Korean"? Do you feel like there's some secret handshake you never got taught? Or a meeting you never got invited to?

You might think the Asian-American kids at UCLA seem like they've got it all figured out. But I'd bet most of them don't. I lived several lifetimes in LA's K-town and I've seen plenty of people pretend like they've always known who they are. That's the trick. No one's really got it figured out. No one feels like a true insider.

Also, neuroscience? Do you cut up brains or something? That sounds like a real major. Like you actually have to work. Respect.

As for the scam, I guess you could try to steal my identity. My credit's wrecked though so scam me at your own peril.

Write if you feel like it.

-James Juwon Shin

Jessica just happened to glance toward the mailboxes as she was running out the door, already late for lab. There it was: another bureaucratic envelope with her name in that same squared-off handwriting, like someone trying to remember how cursive worked. It felt like the response came faster than she anticipated.

Jessica grabbed it and stuffed it into her hoodie pocket, then jogged toward the corner where the Big Blue Bus always came at unpredictable intervals. She read the first line while waiting at the stop. By the time she boarded, she was two paragraphs in.

The bus was packed; standing room only. She held the overhead rail with one hand, the letter with the other. Students jostled around her, backpacks bumping her side, some guy's earbuds leaking the YouTube video he was committed to finishing. But she kept reading.

As she re-read the joke about the scam she could run on him, she missed her stop.

By the time she looked up, the bus had reached North Campus, pulling in front of the law school. She got off, letter still in her hand, and walked slowly back toward South Campus.

She imagined Mr. James Juwon Shin as an old man. Not, like, ancient–but definitely some white in his thinning hair, maybe reading glasses, and possibly a slightly stooped posture. Someone who used to be intense in his youth but had mellowed with time. Someone who had regrets. Who drank weak coffee and told people not to waste their twenties.

Somehow, that made it easier. Safer.

She didn't want to picture tattoos or gang stuff or whatever movies said prison was like. It felt better thinking of him this way–someone who saw through her without trying to impress her, someone who had lived and lost and could offer quiet, slightly judgmental wisdom about her quarter-life identity crisis.

Besides, she wasn't writing for drama. Or danger. Or even excitement.

She just wanted to feel less... alone in this thing.

5.

Dear James,

I'm going to go ahead and assume I am a friend. After all, only friends invite friends to steal their identity. You asked what I meant by "feel Korean." I don't know. I guess because I'm so not Korean, I've kind of given up on being Korean. So instead, I've tried to at least feel Korean. Like maybe that's a lesser version I can attain. It's hard to explain.

I went to this Korean Student Association event on campus–Chusuk? Chuseok? It was in October this year, but someone told me it's in September next year. I tried so hard to learn everything. I stood there listening, nodding, watching how people greeted each other, trying to copy it all in real time like I was cramming for a test.

But I was so stressed, overthinking every little move, that the only thing I actually remember is the taste of song-pyeon. That mochi-like rice cake with the sesame-ish paste inside. Chewy and sweet and a little nutty. For five seconds, I wasn't thinking; I was just eating.

I guess that's like an F in Chuseok, right? Is that a thing people do? Fail at being Korean?

You said you've lived a few lifetimes already. I keep thinking about that. I think I've lived maybe one and a half. How do you know when a lifetime ends and another begins? Like, do you feel it in the moment, or only when you look back?

Also, how old are you, anyway? I assume you must be extremely old to have lived more than a few lifetimes. Maybe prison is your retirement plan after your business ventures went south. My Korean friends say I should show respect to an ahjushi. So-respect.

Update on my plans to ghost you: I think I'll keep writing. You seem... sharp. In a way that makes me want to be a little sharper too.

Your friend,
Minjee
(this is my way of trying to feel a little bit Korean in these letters)

He was sitting on his bunk, legs hanging off the edge, the letter unfolded in his hands. Reading it for the second time. Maybe third. He wasn't counting.

She called herself Minjee now. That made him pause. Signing it seems to be claiming it. And the way she slipped it in at the end–"*this is my way of trying to feel a little bit Korean*"–that hit him harder than he expected. She wasn't trying to land it as a punch, but it still left a mark.

He heard footsteps and snapped the letter closed fast, folding it once with practiced ease just as his cellmate, Luis, leaned in the doorway.

"You still doing that pen-pal thing?" Luis asked, smirking. "College girl got you hooked?"

"It's not like that."

"Mm-hmm. She ask what you're wearing yet?"

"Shut up."

Luis laughed. "You ask what she's wearing? Or–" he made a little camera motion with his fingers, "–you ask for a picture?"

James shook his head. "Nah. That's creepy."

Luis raised an eyebrow. "C'mon. Just a little photo. How else you gonna know if she's a catfish? What if she's a 500 lb, 50-year-old old man who lives in Van Nuys with ten cats?"

"She probably is."

Luis grinned. "Yep. You're just gonna get your identity stolen by an obese dude named Greg."

"Perfect. Then I'll finally have an excuse to stop writing."

They both laughed. The sound echoed in the narrow space between the bunks.

Luis clapped a hand on the doorframe. "Alright, let me know when she sends you instructions on how to transfer Bitcoin."

James waited until he was gone, then pulled the letter out again. Ran his thumb over her name.

Minjee.

Maybe she was a 500-pound old man. Well, he still enjoyed Greg's sense of humor.

6.

Dear Minjee,

Thanks for writing back. Always good to hear from you. Even if you are trying to scam me.

You probably picture me as an old man ahjushi... balding, puttering around as the prison librarian, leaning on a cane. I gotta admit, I've got my own mental image going. I imagine you as a 500-pound, 50-year-old man named Greg from Van Nuys, running a small but successful Bitcoin scam operation out of a room full of cats. My boy Luis is convinced you'll be asking for crypto any day now. So if you were planning to send me your wallet address, now's your chance. It might not be a flattering image, but hey–I'm ready to invest in your cat food empire.

You asked how old I am. I'm 28. So maybe not as ancient as you imagined but prison ages you, fast. It's like dog years in here. You sit still for long enough and suddenly you've got time to inventory every version of yourself you used to be. I didn't realize I'd lived that many lives until I had nothing but time to count them. I had my age of innocence, my scrappy days, my hustling days, my glory days, my epic downfall–and now, I don't know what these days are yet.

So I guess that answers your question: I never know what a lifetime is until I'm past it. A fish swimming in water can't tell you about the water.

You said you've lived one and a half. What were they? And how do you know you're halfway through the second?

Your whole "given up on being Korean and you're just going for feeling Korean"? I gotta call bullshit on that, respectfully. I've been Korean-American my whole life–raised in Koreatown, mom spoke Korean at home, ate Korean food–and I never feel like I'm doing it right. You think I know what Chusuk is? I celebrated it every year as a kid and still couldn't tell you what it's about. All I remember is the food. And yeah, the best part of Chusuk is definitely songpyun. That's the only part I ever cared about. I love that stuff.

Also, no offense, but I don't write "songpyeon." That eo thing always looks weird to me. Nobody says songpyeeeon. You say songpyun. I'm not fancy when I don't need to be.

If the only thing you know about Chusuk is songpyun, congrats. You're as Korean as I am.

You said you'd ghost me after the fourth letter. You've only sent three so far. So, you know... you might still be right on track.

Write when you feel like it.

–James

Minjee let out a sharp, sudden laugh. "Oh my God," she gasped, clutching her stomach. "Greg from Van Nuys! He thinks I'm Greg from Van Nuys!" She curled instinctively into herself, knees tucked up under her oversized UCLA hoodie, rocking back and forth on the old tweed couch. Her leggings stretched as she folded tighter, laughter spilling out in uneven bursts. A strand of hair clung to her cheek where a tear rolled down, the kind that came from laughing too hard and too long.

The image of it–James in prison, picturing her as a 500-pound, 50-year-old man surrounded by cats and cryptocurrency–it was ridiculous. And perfect. And the way he wrote it? Completely deadpan. Like he wouldn't even be surprised. Like he'd accepted that possibility and still wanted to write her back.

Her stomach still hurt from laughing when Rosalie walked in, iced coffee in one hand and a stack of mail in the other.

"Okay, who's Greg?" Rosalie asked, eyebrow raised.

Minjee, still chucking, wiped the corners of her eyes with the cuff of her hoodie.

"Greg," she said, holding up the letter like a piece of evidence, "is me."

Rosalie walked over slowly, like she wasn't sure whether to laugh or stage an intervention.

"Should I be worried?"

Minjee grinned. "Only if I start asking people to wire me Bitcoin. James thinks I'm a scammer named Greg. He imagines that I'm a 500-pound man running a cat-filled Bitcoin scam operation. Honestly, I love that for me."

Rosalie set her iced coffee on the windowsill and sank into the opposite armchair. "Okay, but seriously. What is this now? The second letter in a couple of weeks?"

"The third," Minjee said, then paused. "The third letter in three weeks."

Rosalie gave her a look.

"What?"

"I don't know, Jessica. It's just... you're laughing so hard you're crying over a guy in federal prison. That's kind of... concerning."

Minjee folded the letter once, gently. "He's just... funny. Like, unexpectedly funny. He says weirdly thoughtful things. Maybe the fact that he's a stranger who doesn't know anything about me gives him... I don't know, special insight."

Rosalie leaned back. "And he's how old again?"

"Twenty-eight." Minjee didn't need to look back at the letter. She had instantly updated her image of him.

Another look. Slower, quieter this time.

"I know how it sounds," Minjee said, softer now. "But it's not... it's not like that. It's just... letters. It's just nice."

Rosalie raised her iced coffee and sipped without responding right away.

"Okay," she said finally. "But just... be careful, okay?"

Minjee nodded. "I am."

There was a pause, long enough for the room to settle.

Then Rosalie smirked. "So exactly how much crypto can Greg get out of him?"

Minjee smiled. "Let's see."

7.

Dear James,

Thank you for being so open with your personal information. I'm currently exploring two scam options:

1.	Steal your identity and impersonate you to get 15% off a very expensive bra.

2.	Figure out how to make a Bitcoin wallet and funnel cat food profits directly from federal prison to Van Nuys.

Unfortunately, I don't know how to buy Bitcoin (something about a blockchain?), and I only learned that I need a "wallet" for it from you, my potential victim, so identity theft might be more my lane.

Here's my best guess about my 1.5 lives.

Life One: Being a kid who didn't know anything about anything. Nashville suburbs. White parents. White neighbors. White winter jackets. NPR's Car Talk and lots of books and casseroles. It was a good childhood. But so white that I never talked about how white it was. It was only when I got teased that I'd so clearly feel... not white.

I didn't have the words for it then, so I just smiled and tried to be likeable. Tried so hard to ignore race. If I never acknowledged race, wouldn't it cease to affect me?

Life Two (the .5 part, in progress): Trying to figure out what it means that I'm not white. It's very experimental and mostly jarring. It's so crazy how much the non-white people here just call it out when things are white! My roommates and besties are Latina (half-Mexican, half-Puerto Ri-

*can), Chinese (via Hong Kong), Taiwanese, Singaporean
(like actually from Singapore)... and they talk about it all
the time!*

*So far I've signed up to take an Asian-American history
class next quarter, eaten some songpyun (notice: leaving
out the eo!), listened to my roommates talk about race and
culture stuff at the most random times, and written to a
possibly real Korean-American man in federal prison.*

*I'm not sure what the theme of this second life is going
to be. Mostly, right now, it's defined in contrast to the first
life.*

*Okay, your turn. You mentioned your age of innocence,
your scrappy days, hustling, glory, downfall... can you start
from the beginning? What was your age of innocence like?
How old were you? Why do you now see it as your age of innocence?*

Your friend,
Greg (aka Minjee)

James was lying on his bunk, legs propped up on the wall,
opening up the letter. He instantly scrunched his face. Re-
flexive. Sharp.

He hadn't thought about bras in a long time. Not really.
Not in the way that stayed with you. And he wasn't sure if
he should–not in here, not with her. This letter thing was
supposed to be... harmless. Word-based. Safe.

But goddamn, if she was young and beautiful–in a bra?

He let the thought hang for half a second. Then shoved it
out of his head.

He was kind of endeared to her now. Genuinely. And he didn't want to think about her like that. Not just because it felt wrong–but because it felt... small. Like it would shrink everything good about what this was.

He smoothed out the creases absent mindedly as he re-read the whole thing. She was a kid. She was nice. She was just figuring things out.

But she had to say bra of all things.

Greg, he thought. *You asshole.*

But he was smiling.

8.

Dear Minjee,
Okay. Let me say this in my most ahjushi voice: If you're a teenage college girl writing to a man in federal prison, maybe–and I mean maybe–don't lead with bras.

Dear Greg,
If you're a 50-year-old man trying to scam guys in prison, come on. Bras? Really? That's too obvious. That's Amateur Hour.
Besides, Greg, what are the chances someone named James Juwon Shin wants a very expensive bra? Think about the data flags. Think about the bank. That's the kind of transaction that gets frozen instantly. Feels like some intern at Chase is gonna see that charge and go, "Uh... James? You trying to buy a bra?"
You're gonna get caught, Greg. Be better.

To both Minjee and Greg, I do appreciate your creativity in trying to steal my identity, though. That's some dedication. Shows you're putting some real effort into this pen pal thing.
About the lifetimes–I liked how you broke yours down. It's like there's the part where you were in whiteness and didn't name it; and now you're in the part where you're naming the whiteness all over the place. And yeah, you're right. They're always defined in contrast. Fish don't know

what the water is until they've choked on air. That's how I knew my "age of innocence." I never would've called it that while I was in it.

That age was probably during high school–the time in your life when you're just starting to be aware that you're making decisions. Like, you actually remember your thought process. High school was in that weird strip in LA between Hancock Park and K-Town. You had rich kids from the nicer streets west of Crenshaw, and then the immigrant, Black, and ethnic kids from the tiny apartments tucked behind strip malls. We all mixed. Mostly. Sort of.

I was around campus at all hours because I played soccer and basketball. Tried water polo one year. Lasted like three weeks. Turns out trying-not-to-drown-in-Speedos is not my jam. After practices, I stole Skor bars from this tiny Korean liquor store that still exists, I think. I'd buy a Gatorade and sneak a candy bar into my sleeve. But I was always extra polite. Bowed, spoke Korean, used honorifics. They never suspected the well-mannered Korean teen. That kind of thing worked way too well.

I did fine in AP Calc. Had to cheat in AP Stats, which was embarrassing, because that was supposed to be the easier AP math class. Got into K-Town clubs with fake IDs that were basically arts and crafts projects. Got good at laminating for easy cash. Made out with girls I probably didn't deserve. Crammed seven people into my friend's beat-up white Civic. Two in the trunk sometimes. We'd drive like that to parties, blasting music with the windows down like we were invincible.

That was the extent of my badness during my age of innocence. The kind of badness you almost want to confess to because it still feels like a coming-of-age novel, not real crimes. I wasn't a good kid, but I wasn't a bad one either. Just... figuring it out.

    Like you said. Life Two is mostly defined in contrast. Were you ever "bad"? Or is your whole life innocence? Well, you know, except all the scams you are running.

    –James

Minjee always smiled while reading James' letters. But as she re-read the latest one, she winced.

"Oh my gaaawd." She flipped onto her back and groaned into her hoodie sleeve. Her face burned.

She hadn't even thought about it like that. Not really. Not in a "you're a man, I'm a woman, you're in prison and probably haven't seen a woman in ages" kind of way. She just... felt comfortable with him. She wasn't trying to flirt. She wasn't trying to remind him that she had boobs. She genuinely had her eye on a really expensive bra. Eighty dollars! That was like her food budget for two weeks. It had mesh sides and was rated really highly by *Consumer Reports*. Women online claimed it was the only bra they didn't immediately rip off when they got home.

Now she just felt dumb. Not because he'd been mean about it. He hadn't. He'd joked. Gently. He'd given her advice like some semi-retired scam coach who was also sort of worried about her safety. That made it worse, somehow.

What am I even doing? she thought. Writing letters to a man in federal prison like it's a game.

And he is a man. That's the part she hadn't really let herself think through. She'd imagined him old at first. Then wise. Then funny. And somewhere in there, she forgot he was a stranger. A stranger who had lived through whole lifetimes she couldn't even picture. His "age of innocence" had fake IDs and liquor store shoplifting and making out with girls in club bathrooms. Her "bad" phase was... making out with one guy, and thinking about making out with another.

She couldn't tell him that. She barely wanted to admit it to herself. And she had learned the lesson James was trying to teach her–don't talk about making out or anything remotely sexy with guys in prison. She needed James to remind her that she didn't know anything about what it was like to be in prison.

But that was the whole reason she'd started this, right? Because she cared about justice. About humanity. About systems. She'd written to an inmate to prove that all of us were fundamentally human. Children of God. All the same. Equally valuable and worthless in the context of history. But now she was just curled up on a bed, blushing into her hoodie, realizing how little she actually knew about anything.

She groaned again. Louder this time.

Then she reached for her notebook.

9.

Dear James,

You think Greg's been caught? No way, man. I'm an innocent, neurosci co-ed who doesn't even think about men thinking about bras. That's right. Aren't guys super into totally clueless girls? Cue the batting of eyelashes. Greg is playing the long game. This is 4D chess, bro. Psychological warfare. You're already letting your guard down. Get ready for checkmate.

Anyway.

You asked if I've ever been "bad." The short answer is no. And somehow, I kinda feel like a failure about it as I write this letter. My life is probably less interesting because the worst thing I ever did was steal a rocket-shaped lollipop from the 99¢ Store in third grade. (My mom caught me and made me take it back. Mortifying.)

I copied chemistry homework all junior year from Arjun Patel-but to be fair, everyone did. That was basically a rite of passage at our high school. One time our teacher, Mr. Penkala, accused Arjun of copying off me and I started laughing so hard I almost fell off my chair. Arjun's face was so offended. That's when the guys in the class started saying Mr. Penkala had an Asian girl fetish. Ugh.

Everything I know about the badness of the world comes from books.

And if I'm being real with you, your age of innocence sounds like it could be the urban <u>Huck Finn</u>. Or <u>Catcher in</u>

the Rye. But, like, if Holden Caulfield was sneaking into K-Town clubs with a laminated fake ID then judging everyone hard once he got in there. I don't want to romanticize your childhood, but it does kind of seem like a coming-of-age novel I'd stay up all night reading.

How did your "age of innocence" end? I mean, what ended it? What was the moment when the next life started? Tell me about Life Two. The one that came in contrast.

And by the way, this is letter number five. I am officially not ghosting you.

But maybe now you'll ghost me. Because you don't want to tell me about Life Two. Or because I'm too innocent. And don't know anything about anything.

Your friend (and aspiring scam artist),
"Minjee"

James was in the yard doing pull-ups. Controlled. Focused. One movement at a time.

The bar was cold in his hands, rough with chipped paint. He liked the rhythm–up, down, up, down. A set number. A set limit. He liked feeling his lats burn, the way his body stayed hard, the way he'd built something in here that nobody could take from him.

Except his mind kept drifting.

He'd read Minjee's letter that morning. Then re-read it. This time, it had come on wide-ruled notebook paper, the kind with faint red margins and blue lines, with tiny perforations on one side where she'd neatly torn it out. It screamed school. It screamed student. It screamed *young*.

He'd folded it too neatly, too carefully, and tucked it under his mattress with the rest of them.

She really was innocent. And now he knew too much. The lollipop. The copied chem homework. The "Asian girl fetish" comment from high school boys–which, let's be real, they wouldn't have said unless she was attractive. That kind of attractive. The kind white boys in Tennessee call "exotic" and "delicate" and "submissive" without ever saying the words. The kind that ends up on someone's search history. The kind that gets an Asian woman in a pencil skirt bent over a conference table in a boardroom. That kind.

He hadn't been thinking about her that way. Not really. Not consciously. But now? Now it was in the file. Now it was in his brain. Now she wasn't just Minjee/possibly Greg, sarcastic pen pal and scammer extraordinaire. Now she was Minjee who was probably beautiful. Fuckable.

He didn't know how he felt about that. It was too much. Too soon. Too something. He couldn't have thoughts like that. Not in here. Not about her.

If this was a scam, she was good. Really good. She was playing him, but in all the ways that didn't feel like a con. Just subtle. Just one honest story at a time. Like water seeping into the cracks.

But his body betrayed the pace. He knocked out the last few pull-ups harder than he needed to. Dropped to the ground, chest heaving, arms shaking, skin galvanized with sweat and something else that wasn't there before.

Letters were supposed to be safe. Letters were supposed to be slow. He wasn't supposed to feel like this.

10.

Dear Minjee (or Greg),

First of all, your innocent life? Not boring. That's the kind of stuff people end up wishing for. You know what's actually wild? People who go to college. Who major in neuroscience. Who know what a ganglion cell is. Who walk around campus in college-branded hoodies with twenty pounds of textbooks, getting unsolicited offers from guys to carry them. That's romantic in the classic sense. Not <u>Romeo and Juliet</u>, but, like, Jane Austen. Proper. Dignified. A little tension around the edges, but mostly sweet.

I'm no Holden Caulfield. I wasn't standing around the club sneering at the phonies–I was the ultimate phony. Drinking champagne and partying with the people he would've written essays about.

Okay. Story time: Life One was my age of innocence but here's how it ended.

I was supposed to go to Williams. Got in with a decent scholarship. But then my mom got sick. Like, sick sick. We didn't know what it was for months. Just that she was in a lot of pain and doctors kept shrugging and running tests. Eventually, it was pancreatic cancer. Stage 4. The pain was constant. Sharp. I watched her fold in on herself like something was eating her from the inside out–which it was. This marked the start of Life Two.

I never left for Massachusetts. Started community college nearby so I could get her to appointments, manage the *house, keep things afloat. Medical bills stacked like library books. So I started hustling a little. Oxy at first. For her. For pain. Then for others. Then for money. Then Molly, Special K, a little LSD. I had a knack for it. Customer-oriented, reliable, discreet. Word spread.*

Before long, I was supplying to guys who got bottle service in LA clubs. Some of them brought K-pop idols and actors with them when they visited LA. I started to know names. Faces. Drivers. Personal assistants. Hosts. That was the beginning of the money.

But I didn't keep any of it. Every single cent went to my mom.

I didn't party. I didn't spend. I went to doctor visits. Slept in waiting rooms. Learned how to argue with billing departments. Tried to finish assignments in hospital cafeterias or on her bedside table. Eventually, I stopped doing the assignments. And then I stopped going to class altogether.

Everything was about her. Everything was her. And then one day, it wasn't. That's how Life Two ended.

I could apologize for such a sad letter, but that'd be like you apologizing for your sweet, innocent, awesome life. This isn't a contest. It's just... stories. We're just trading stories. I'm thankful for your stories and I hope you enjoy getting mine.

Even if you are Greg, I like getting your letters. I hope you keep writing back.

-James

Minjee had been carrying James's letter in the back pocket of her jeans all day. She hadn't opened it during class. Didn't read it while waiting for the bus. She wanted to wait. Wanted a moment.

Now, Powell Library was nearly empty. The sky outside the bay windows had gone that particular UCLA shade of dusk–soft lavender sliding onto gold. The padded bench beneath her creaked as she shifted, letter already unfolded in her lap. All around her, the heavy books on the shelves leaned in like they were listening too.

She read slowly. Like the weight of it demanded it.

She read about his mom. About the pain. About the dealing and the hospitals and the money he didn't keep. She read about Life Two starting not with rebellion or some wild decision–but with love. And ultimately, loss.

And then she just sat there, the letter soft in her hands, the air outside dimming, the library silent except for a distant page turning somewhere else.

She felt the weight of it. Not just the story, but his tone. The shift in it. It felt like he became somehow more real. And he let her in.

She thought about how much she didn't know. About pain. About loss. Real loss.

Her own childhood had been quiet. Gentle. She hadn't lost her birth parents so much as... never known them. She didn't remember the loss, so sometimes it didn't feel real. It was like something that had happened in the prologue of her life. Someone else's chapter.

But James had known his mom. Had loved her. Had watched her go piece by piece.

She couldn't imagine losing college. Losing home. Losing her.

She folded the letter back slowly, carefully. Her fingers ran over the creased edge. James wasn't just a pen pal anymore. He wasn't even a stranger. He was someone who'd trusted her with something sacred.

This letter came from him. He touched it. And he was a real person.

11.

Dear James,

Thank you for telling me about your mom. About Life Two.

That can't have been an easy story to write. I read it slowly, like it deserved to be read. I don't know how to say this without sounding sentimental, but... thank you for trusting me with that part of you.

I've never had a loss like that. At least not one I remember. I think the biggest loss of my life happened before I had words for it. But your letter made me think about what it means to really be aware of losing someone. To carry it with you, day by day, until one day there's nothing left to carry. Just absence. Just the after.

And also–Williams? Are you kidding me? That school is hard to get into. Like... "future senator on the national fencing team" hard. You were clearly the overachieving type, despite your penchant for fake IDs (or perhaps those skills were parlayed into college admissions). Color me impressed.

You're wrong about one thing: your letter wasn't sad. It was alive. And I know that sounds weird, but it didn't feel like a wound. It felt like a person–like you. Not some dramatic story about pain, but a life that kept going even when it didn't want to.

I thought about that letter for a while. I carried it around like a talisman. I want to hear about Life Three.

I'm going back to Nashville for winter break, so if you send a letter, I might not get it for a few weeks. Merry Christmas and Happy New Year.

Your friend (and a true failure at scamming),

Minjee

James waited until Christmas morning to open the letter.

He'd had it for two days. Gotten it later than expected. Long enough for the ache to start.

He hadn't realized how much he'd gotten used to the rhythm—how her letters had started to carve time into something steady. Every few days, a piece of her arrived. And this time, when it didn't? He felt it. Like a weight in his chest. Like something had sagged that he couldn't name.

He saw the Tennessee postmark right away. And just like that, his heart sat up. Like a bored kid slouched at his desk, suddenly realizing it was worth paying attention.

He knew, then. He was in trouble.

He wasn't supposed to fall for a pen pal. He wasn't some tragic cliché. She wasn't ever going to fall for him. That wasn't how this worked. He was just setting himself up for a world of pain.

If a few delayed days of mail already ached like that... what the hell was he going to do when she moved on? When she graduated? Got busy? Got a boyfriend? Filed the letters away in a box somewhere and forgot they ever meant anything?

He unfolded her letter carefully, hands too steady. Read it once. Then again.

He felt that telltale heaviness in his chest. That tug. Like he was going over a cliff. Like water rushing him toward a fall he couldn't stop. He needed to pull back. He had to pull back.

He couldn't let himself linger over her words. He couldn't smile at the paper like some shy kid getting his first real compliment. He couldn't believe she saw the scrappy kid sleeping in a hospital chair. He couldn't believe she said he was real. And he definitely couldn't believe she was real.

Not like that.

Because if she was real, and she saw him... then what?

12.

Dear Minjee/Greg,

Let's just say that this is all a scam. That you're some fat guy sitting in his mother's basement with a bunch of crypto tabs open, laughing your ass off while writing "Merry Christmas" and neuroscience jokes in cursive.

Honestly? I hope that's the truth.

Because the alternative–that you're real, and you mean what you write–is too hard. And I'm not sure how I'll feel when you're done with the letter writing phase of your life.

So here we go. Life Three.

After my mom died, I wanted to buy her a plot in Forest Lawn. The best I could afford. Somewhere that felt real. Respectful. The kind of place she never got to live in while she was alive. The first time I visited, I found one I could swing. It was off to the side of a service road, near a retaining wall. Nothing fancy. But the plaque was bronze. Clean. Modest. Like something she would've picked out for someone else. Never for herself.

I didn't have serious money yet. But that's the moment I decided I'd get it.

I started treating the business like a business. Called in all the favors. All the contacts I'd made during Life Two: the club guys, the big spenders, the personal assistants, the visiting celebrities. I became the guy who always had the cleanest, strongest, smoothest high, and always delivered right before you even thought to want it.

I knew the rhythm of the clubs. I knew when people would be craving the next hit. I knew which girls would get past security. I hired delivery girls-smart, stunning, professional. A scheduler. A kid who did the books and ended up majoring in computer science at Berkeley. I studied spreadsheets during the day and networked the clubs at night.

I got a downtown apartment. Sleek. Fully furnished. Barely stayed there, except when I needed to convince someone new to come work for me. I drove a series of BMWs. Each more expensive than the last. Never flashy. Always smooth. Elegant. My clothes got sharper. My contacts got bigger.

One client, a Hong Kong guy named Kee, started talking about being my mentor. An investor. That moment was also the beginning of the end. But I didn't know it at the time. There was a whole life left to go before the downfall.

But I'll stop here for now. Gotta end on a cliffhanger, so you'll write back.

Tell me more about you. How's Nashville? What does it feel like to be home again? Do your parents know about these letters? Are you calling them "white" all the time now? Are you sleeping in your childhood bed with old stuffed animals in the corner?

And neuroscience-how did you end up in that major? I still don't understand what a ganglion cell is. (Do I even have one?)

Also, why are you writing to someone like me? I mean, even though I got into Williams, I didn't go. Ended up dealing party drugs and losing the person I loved most. What makes you write letters to a lame prisoner like me?

Greg, you are truly an asshole. This is such a long con.
And I'm such a sucker for falling for it.
*   -James*

Minjee sat at the breakfast nook in her childhood home, elbows tucked in, legs covered in soft flannel curled up under her chair like she used to sit when she was ten. Her dad sat across from her in his usual seat, *The Tennessean* folded wide in front of him, a half-drunk cup of coffee beside his phone.

It was early, quiet. The kind of quiet that felt arranged. Like a Norman Rockwell painting with central air. Except Minjee never felt like her face quite fit in the frame.

She unfolded James' letter at the table, the creases soft from how many times she'd already read it. Her eyes skimmed down to the end. Where he calls her, or rather Greg, an asshole.

She let out a soft laugh, right into her mug. Then, immediately, there it was—that pang. The way he wrote falling for it. As if falling for her—or Greg—was the worst kind of mistake.

His letters made her feel more like herself than anything else had in years. Even though half of every letter was spent denying she existed.

Across the table, her dad looked up. Salt-and-pepper hair, glasses low on his nose. He was still in a dress shirt even though it was Saturday. VP of a regional bank. Member of the Kiwanis club (currently raising money for filariasis, a disease no one in their zip code could spell). Rational. Kind.

A man who believed in discipline, compound interest, and private school applications.

"Who's the letter from?" he asked, setting the paper down.

Minjee didn't look up right away. "Oh. Just this guy."

Her dad raised an eyebrow. "I know I'm being a total cliché dad here," he said, a smile playing at the corners of his mouth, "but... what are his intentions?"

She grinned. "No intentions. He doesn't believe I'm real."

That got both eyebrows. "You've never met?"

Minjee shrugged. "Yeah. We're pen pals."

He leaned back slightly. "Like a college exchange program or something?"

There was a beat. Then she lied. "Yeah. With students from Williams College."

His face lit up a little even while his eyes returned to his paper. "Good school. Perhaps the best liberal arts college in the country."

She nodded, eyes still on the letter. "Doesn't matter. I'll never meet him."

One of his brows furrowed. "You seem to be enjoying the letter."

Minjee looked up. "Yeah," she said softly. And then, before she could stop herself, "I am."

13.

Dear James,

Season's greetings from Nashville! Where cur Norman Rockwell "super-white" Christmas included daily coffee at the kitchen table with my dad, a candlelight service at my parents' church, and the annual game of who brought the best pie. (I won. By cheating. I made chess pie from a <u>New York Times</u> cookbook. Don't tell anyone from my church that this was a YANKEE liberal pie.)

I told my dad (kind of) about you. He asked what your intentions were. I said you were a pen pal who didn't believe I existed. I didn't mention the part where you're writing from prison. But honestly, I think I've learned more from your letters than from any class at UCLA. I don't remember a single thing from linear algebra.

Why am I a neuroscience major? I thought I'd go pre-med at first but now, as a senior (hey, I'm not a teenager!), I'm not so sure. I'm doing research in a psychobio lab, training rats to find Fruit Loops in mazes and then looking at their hippocampus under a microscope. Isn't it wild that the same squishy, slimy stuff that helps a rat chase sugar also lets us write letters? Solve equations? Read <u>Ulysses</u>? (Well, some of us.)

You once joked about me cutting up brains. I literally slice them into very thin samples and stain them. It's exactly as macabre as it sounds. (Would Greg make up this *much bloody detail? Do you finally believe I'm not catfishing you? How would this even be part of a scam?)*

Oh and FYI: You have a bunch of ganglion cells in your eyeballs.

And maybe because I'm feeling a little lost–about not being Korean enough, about letting go of med school–I've come to really appreciate this letter-writing thing. I signed up half-doubting anyone would write back. But I thought maybe if I did this, it would prove something: that we're fundamentally the same. Not better, not worse. Not lost, not found.

I think I'm bullshitting at this point.

By the way, Life Three was wild: the clubs, the BMWs, the girl-recruiting penthouse (okay... wow). It's the <u>Rocky</u> training montage of a party-drug CEO, I guess. The makeover moment where you go from scrappy kid to Jay Gatsby–except your lavish parties swapped the jazz orchestra for flawless pill logistics and hot girls with clipboards. Feels like something between <u>Breaking Bad</u> and <u>The Devil Wears Prada</u>.

I wish I could've seen the rise.

But what really gets me is the contrast between Life Two and Life Three. There's ash and loss in Two. But then somehow you transformed in Three. There's a part of me that wishes you had already sent me Life Four, but I think it's better that it's coming one letter at a time.

When I read your letters, I don't feel like I'm watching someone spiral or redeem themselves. I feel like I'm witnessing someone being built. One life at a time.

Your friend,

Minjee, a true asshole
P.S. Write back to me at my UCLA address. School's starting up soon.

James was working in the library–stacking returns, checking out paperbacks, answering the same three questions he always got: "You got that book from the movie?" "You got anything with pictures?" "You got something short?"

The prison library wasn't big. Fluorescent lights. One broken window that whined in the wind. The books had barcodes half-torn and corners chewed up like they'd lived other lives. But it was quiet. And quiet was a kind of currency.

He was reshelving when his eyes landed on <u>The Great Gatsby</u>.

He hesitated. Then pulled it out. Checked it out to himself.

Later, after the count, he sat on his bunk and flipped it open. Minjee's letter was tucked between the pages, carefully folded, like it had always belonged there. Like it was its own kind of story.

He read the letter again. Slower this time. He didn't skim. He listened.

When he got to the Gatsby line, he laughed under his breath.

The makeover moment where you go from scrappy kid to Jay Gatsby-except your lavish parties swapped the jazz or-

chestra for flawless pill logistics and hot girls with clip-boards.

It was absurd. And accurate.

He had met college girls back then. Girls with shiny hair and practiced irony. Girls who said they loved molly but never paid for it. Girls who'd smile at him in the club like they knew a secret he didn't.

But he had a feeling he never would've met her. His circles just didn't overlap with someone like Minjee. Someone who would write long, loopy letters to an inmate. Someone who wanted Life One. Then Life Two. And even Life Three.

She told her dad. About him. It had been a long time since a girl introduced him to her father. Maybe ever.

He should ask whether she has a boyfriend.

No. That's ridiculous. It doesn't matter.

She could have one. She should have a real one. Someone from her linear algebra class. Someone who brings her coffee at her lab. Not some has-been Jay Gatsby. In prison.

He sighed and leaned back on his bed, simultaneously flipping open the The Great Gatsby above him. Maybe he just needed to escape into someone else's tragedy for a few pages.

He just stared at the words.

There must have been moments even that afternoon when Daisy tumbled short of his dreams–not through her own fault but because of the colossal vitality of his illusion.

He read it twice. Three times.

And all he could think was: *I wish Greg–the colossally vital illusion–was real.*

Because his Daisy–if she could even be called that–wasn't falling short of the dream. She was outpacing it. Outrunning it. Writing letters with more depth than he'd expected from any real person, let alone some half-imagined scammer.

It wasn't the colossal vitality of his illusion.

It was the colossal vitality of his *reality*.

That was what scared him. Because reality also meant this: He was in prison. She was not.

14.

To Greg, my dearest asshole,

You know, I don't get tripped up by your bloody neuroscience details. I know you just looked that shit up, but those details are GOLD, man. That's what makes it all so believable. I truly wish your cat food empire the best. You deserve it.

Dear Minjee,

So you bake award-winning pies, huh? There's a part of me that wishes I could taste them. But that part is overpowered by the part of me that wants to make fun of you for being so white. What the hell is chess pie? If you ever want to be accepted into the secret Korean meeting, never mention chess pie. We'll revoke your kimchi privileges on the spot.

You're not pre-med anymore? So what is in store for you post-college? Some noble nonprofit? Science for the sake of science?

It was weird imagining you talking about me with your dad. Your life sounds... old-fashioned. A caring father at the kitchen table, asking about a man's intentions for his daughter? That's some Emma *shit. Honestly, it's kind of sweet. I'm glad you have a dad who cares about you.*

I checked out The Great Gatsby *in honor of your letter. From the prison library. That guy is truly an asshole. But so was I. Especially during Life Three.*

You ready for Life Four?

Minjee was sitting cross-legged on her bed, the slightly stiff institutional paper hanging from her hand like a treasure map with no X.

She flipped it over... Blank.

She squinted back into the envelope. Tilted it. Shook it... Nothing.

"Are you kidding me?" she muttered.

She stared at the final line again: *"You ready for Life Four?"*

Then nothing. No story. No beginning. No new chapter.

She audibly growled as she crumpled the letter in her hands. "WHERE THE HELL IS LIFE FOUR?" she said out loud, to no one in particular.

She wanted to tear up the letter–in something that looked like rage but felt way too much like longing. It was absurd. She was sitting in a cramped Westwood apartment, losing her mind over a guy in federal prison who had the audacity to give her Jay Gatsby with BMWs and club girls–and then stop right before the next act.

And yet.

She uncrumpled it. Smoothed it out. Folded it neatly again and tucked the letter back in the envelope.

She flopped back on her bed.

Fine. Two can play the long game.

15.

James smirked before he even opened the envelope.

He thought he'd been slick–ending the last letter with "*You ready for Life Four?*" and just walking away. It had taken all the restraint he had not to peek over his shoulder, not to drop another sentence, not to give her exactly what he knew she wanted.

Teasing her was becoming his favorite game.

So when the letter arrived–same thin paper, same neat fold–he settled in with that smug, preemptive grin already forming.

He unfolded it.

JAMES!

You are such a tease.

I was almost all the way there. But you stopped just when it was getting good.

You know you're driving me a little crazy, right?

Just give it to me already.

I want it. Bad.

-MC

He froze.

It felt physical. Like someone flicked a nerve just under his skin. His chest tightened. His jaw clenched. He wasn't sure if he needed to laugh or run a lap or take a cold shower.

He swallowed hard and folded the letter slowly, too carefully. No one could see this letter.

What the hell had he started?

Now he heard her voice–close, warm, wired into him–saying, "*I want it. <u>Bad</u>.*" He couldn't unhear it. He was going to hear it in his dreams. He was fucked.

Part 2

Seoul

Present Day

T he dog was barking again.

Not a warning bark. A performance bark. Shrill. Like he needed everyone in a five-block radius to know a leaf had fallen or an empty soda bottle had dared to exist. It was a constant in the background now, just above the buzz of the drone controller and the rumble of the ladder truck adjusting its angle.

He squinted up at the 26th floor of the shiny high-rise, watching the pallet of shrink-wrapped furniture inch toward the target balcony's sliding doors. The trick was the rotation. Off by two degrees and the sofa frame would scrape the railing or get wedged in the steel door frame. Then you'd have to lower it again and recalibrate, which wasted time and looked amateur. And that was not happening on his watch.

"(Little more to the left)," he said into the mic. "(Good, now rotate five degrees clockwise. Yep. There. Stop.)"

The operator made the adjustment. The load glided cleanly through the open glass panel and disappeared into the apartment.

He exhaled, finally, and sipped his coffee.

Behind him, Rob, a jet-lagged global strategy exec from the States, clapped him on the back. "You guys made this so easy. My wife didn't know it could be done in a single day. While she's out shopping. Amazing."

He laughed easily and nodded. Americans appreciated this kind of thing. That was the whole business model. Seamless. Effortless. Big machines and tight logistics. Get in, get out, get paid. And he made sure to speak in all the familiar idioms: *no problem at all, you're all set, we'll take it from here.* He knew how to make them feel at ease. Taken care of. They didn't just think the job was handled; they felt like he was a one-man welcome wagon.

The dog barked again, closer this time. He turned just in time to see a blur of tiny fur and unnecessary enthusiasm dart under the ladder truck.

"*Sehkki* (little bastard)," he muttered. "Ya! Get out of there!" He scanned the sidewalk for Dohee.

The dog emerged proudly with something in his mouth. Possibly a ginko nut, possibly one of Rob's expensive cufflinks. Hard to say.

"Argh, I should have named him Rocket, not Frodo!" Dohee called out, exasperated. "He's the worst!"

She jogged up, long dark braid swinging behind her, and scooped the dog up with practiced ease, tucking him under one arm. Frodo yapped once more in protest, then surrendered, tongue out.

He shook his head, grinning despite himself.

Of all the mistakes he'd made in his life, bringing home that ridiculous little dog wasn't the worst. Especially not when he remembered the look on her face. Kneeling in the shop, hugging him like a prize, already calling him Frodo. And the way her little brother had lost his mind when they brought him through the door.

He once thought he could say no to things like that. Now? Not a chance.

Lompoc/Los Angeles – 2012

16.

Dear MC,

You really shouldn't write things like that to a man in federal prison. I'm just saying. There are rules. Social norms. Ethical boundaries. I'm pretty sure "I want it. <u>Bad</u>." violates all of them.

Because now I hear it. Your voice. Over and over. I wake up to it.

So... Yeah. Thanks for that.

Did you know what you were doing when you wrote that? That's a real question. Because part of me wants to believe you were just messing around, playing back the tease. Part of me thinks, "Of course she knows," because you're too damn clever. And part of me just... hopes you don't know.

I guess I'd better start talking about Life Four.

Life Four is legally hard to talk about. These are the details that got me here. I'll tell you what I can. What's indisputable.

I met Kee.

Kee thought I had promise. He invested in my business. I started modeling it after McDonald's or maybe more like Chick-fil-A: franchisees. They'd buy in and get my supply, my brand, my database infrastructure, my scheduling strategies. They got the HR side too–how to vet and recruit girls who could walk into a club, make a delivery, and never raise an eyebrow.

I had franchisees in major U.S. cities with sizable Asian populations. It took a few thousand miles on budget airlines but it was great to see if my ideas could work in a new city.

I stepped back from the LA operation and focused on lo-gistics. Training. Systems.

I wasn't in clubs anymore. I was sleeping normal hours. I felt like a real businessman.

And then–bam. Interstate transport. The DEA. A sting.

I can't say more.

But those were the glory days. Not because of the flash. Not because of the BMWs or the tailored suits or the beau-tiful employees. But because I felt grown.

I was up early. Figuring out pricing. Coordinating sched-ules. Reading business books (not ironically). Mentoring younger guys just starting out. Trying to keep them from blowing it all on cars, on girls, on ego.

An old girlfriend even dragged me to church during those days. That's how clean I was living.

I actually cooked in that downtown apartment. (Not a penthouse, by the way. Just a nice two-bedroom. Two bath-rooms, though. I was living large.) I worked out regularly. I thought about getting a dog.

Sometimes I think–if we had ever met... I wish you'd met me then.

–James

Minjee sat open mouthed. The letter was closed on her lap but his words buzzed low and electric under her skin.

Because now I hear it. Your voice. Over and over. I wake up to it.

He wakes up to it? She blinked. Oh God. She felt suddenly frozen. Like her blood stopped moving.

Wasn't that what she wanted? For him to feel frustrated? For him to feel like she felt? But now she understood. What that frustration was. What he wanted.

He wanted *her.*

She wrote that letter in a heat. In a blur. She had been frustrated. Teased, wound up, a little undone. And she wanted to drive him crazy, the way he was driving her.

But this was it. This was a man driven crazy. A man in federal prison. A man who couldn't stop hearing her voice. A man who woke up to it.

And it hit her, all at once, that there was no version of this that existed in real life. Not the version they'd built. Not the thing with the jokes about Greg. Not the story-swapping across lifetimes. Not the spaces between the stories. Not this tender, aching rhythm they'd fallen into.

They could never have had this in real life. Holden Caulfield with the fake IDs, Emma's dad, and Gatsby couldn't exist in the sunlight.

What they had was only possible in the slcw dribble of ink on paper.

And what had this even become? What *was* this?

17.

Dear James,

Okay.

So... maybe I didn't entirely think through the consequences of that last letter.

I was writing in a very particular emotional state (read: slightly unhinged), and I think I had this fantasy that you'd just sort of... Laugh? Tease me back? Feel guilty about not giving me Life Four?

Instead you said: "Because now I hear it. Your voice. Over and over. I wake up to it."

And yeah. Ahem. Let me think... what am I trying to say...

Part of me wanted that reaction, I won't lie. I wanted to get to you. But now that I have, now that I know I did, I'm just sitting here blinking at the page like, "Oh. Right. This is a real man. With real skin. And real mornings."

But the truth is, you've never actually heard my voice. You don't know what I sound like. Not really. You might just be imagining Greg's voice.

There's a part of me that wants to walk it back. Say "just kidding," go back to talking about ganglion cells and chess pie. There's a part of me that wants to press rewind.

But then I flip back to the part of me that wrote that letter in the first place. And although that part is still stunned... it's also kind of glad to know I can drive you a little bit crazy.

So yeah. No regrets. But maybe... just a little caution.
Still friends?
Minjee
P.S. What would have happened if we met during Life Four?

The letter rested on his knee.

This one didn't hit like the last one. It didn't make him clench his jaw or press his hands into his knees.

This one was worse. Because this one was tender.

She was glad she could drive him a little crazy. She knew now. Knew the effect she had on him. Knew she could pull the string. And she didn't run from it. She just held it. Gently.

He'd never wanted to be sweet. He wasn't innocent. That wasn't the life he'd trained for. But reading this letter, he wished he could be.

He wished he'd taken a different path. Opened boba shops or nail salons. Met her at a dog park in Koreatown. Or at the Central Library, both reaching for The Great Gatsby, both insisting the other take the well-worn copy.

He'd take her to get *galbi jjim* (braised beef short ribs), then walk her to a market that sold *songpyeon* by the kilo, wrapped tight in styrofoam with cling wrap. He'd meet her at LACMA and pretend to know something about Asian ceramics while she laughed at him for mispronouncing *celadon*. He'd buy her bacon-wrapped hot dogs from the street vendors and they'd sit on the grass telling each other the stories of their lives.

He'd bring her coffee when she was working late in the lab, even if she smelled like rat brains. (He had no idea what rat brains smelled like.) He'd pay the absurd UCLA parking fees just to drop it off. Just to see her face when she opened the door.

But that wasn't his life.

His life was this: a quiet cell, a folded letter, a girl who didn't belong in his world getting closer than anyone ever had. He'd let it go too far. He thought the danger was in the wanting. But this was worse. It was being wanted back.

He couldn't give her anything. But she should have *everything*.

So he'd say the thing that would make her stop. Because someone had to set her free. And she might not do it herself. He'd do what needed to be done. Even if it meant breaking the only real connection he'd had in years. Even if it meant breaking himself.

18.

Dear Minjee,

You know... you're kind of impossible. You are worse than Greg. Greg just wanted my Bitcoin. What is it that you want from me? Because the truth is–you have it.

I don't want to but I think about you.

Your voice. (Which I haven't heard.)

Your face. (Which I haven't seen.)

You.

And I think about what it would've been like to meet you in real life. When I looked like someone you could introduce to your friends. When I looked like someone who could walk into your lab and hand you coffee. When I still had time.

But that's not my life.

I know you're not a teenager, but you're still young. You're at UCLA. You've got rat brains to slice. You've got dreams to chase. You've got midterms to bomb and all-nighters to pull and boys to meet. You should write letters to someone who could meet your parents, eat songpyun with you, and French kiss you behind the stacks in the library.

I'm not that person.

I am a guy in prison. For a just reason. And when this is over, I might not be here at all. And while I'm writing you letters and imagining who I could've been, you're out there actually being someone. Don't waste your last year of col-

lege on me. You don't owe me that. Even if, somehow, I've become a little more yours than I meant to be.

You're real, Minjee. And I'm... in here.

Don't wait for this. Don't wait for me. Don't write back.

–James

Minjee didn't cry when she opened the envelope. She didn't cry when she saw the familiar handwriting. She didn't know she started crying until a tear fell straight onto *"Don't write back."*

But it didn't smudge the ink. Ballpoint doesn't run. Not when it's written neat and careful, with the squarish edges James always used. Like every word needed its own space.

She held the letter for a long time. Then, without thinking too hard, she unzipped her backpack and plucked out a page from her spiral notebook without taking it out. The edges ran ragged from the spirals.

She scribbled out.

You're right. I am real. Do you want me to send you a picture?

She stared at the words on the notebook page for a beat. Then she tore it up.

She ran upstairs to her apartment. The late February air bit at her skin as she turned into the exposed walkway. Everything felt too bright, too loud, too ordinary.

She dug through her desk drawer, pulled out a flat box of random paper and receipts and ticket stubs. At the bottom, she found it. One of those photo booth strips from a friend's wedding. Her friends had run out of the last frame. And she was left laughing. Really laughing.

She cut the photo. Left only the frame with her in it. No note. No message.

Just a face. Just her. Proof.

She slipped it into a plain envelope. Wrote *James Juwon Shin, FCI Lompoc* with neat, careful letters. No return address.

She dropped it in the mailbox before she could change her mind.

Then she walked to the library. Fast. Like the act might catch up with her if she didn't outrun it.

19.

He stared at the envelope.

He thought he wouldn't hear from her again. He'd hoped not to. Even though the thought nearly killed him, he'd hoped she'd go out drinking, make out with a stranger, and forget him.

But here it was. *James Juwon Shin, FCI Lompoc* in her now-familiar handwriting.

Should he open it? Something about the weight felt off. Not light. Not right. No letter, probably. The dimensions were wrong. Too thin. Too still.

He opened it anyway. Tipped it slightly. Held it open wider with his hand. And it fell out.

A photo.

Devastating.

A luminous girl in a classic black dress, a chunky orange necklace at her collarbone. Glossy black hair, flipped out and bouncy. Chestnut eyes shining. A full pink mouth caught in the middle of an even fuller laugh, clapping her hands at something just off the edge of the frame.

Alive. Mid-breath. Unapologetically real.

20.

Greg,
 Are you trying to kill me?
 –James

She let out a breath she didn't know she'd been holding. Laughed. A real, unguarded, out-loud laugh.

Then she pressed the paper to her chest and kept walking.

Relieved. And something else, too.

21.

Dear James,

So... you liked the picture?

Just wondering. You did say "Don't write back." And technically, I didn't. But somehow, sending you that photo still got you to write back. Even though you basically told me to go make out with a poli sci major in cargo shorts. Or a condescending TA. Or maybe I should get catfished on OKCupid. You think that's what I want?

I don't want any of it.

Right now, I just want this. These letters. The weird honesty of it. The slow drip of story.

You.

Besides, you still owe me Life Five, the downfall. No teasing. No withholding. You just tell me what happens next. I'm already invested in the story.

Yours,

Minjee

P.S. Just for the record: Greg was absolutely not trying to kill you. He just wants you to believe in something real.

This girl.

James stared at the letter, shaking his head like it might clear the fog in his chest. But clearly, it didn't work.

Because there it was, plain as day, at the bottom of the page: *Yours.*

It was like the word had its own light. Not like a bright pinpoint of light. But like a gentle lifting of the grays and blacks in a tunnel where there is a source of light around the corner but you can't quite see it yet.

He'd written it without meaning to. That he was hers. Or at least more hers than he meant to be. More than he was trying to let on. But it snuck out onto the page.

And she'd written back: *Yours.*

Somewhere in his frontal lobe, a desperate voice tried to be reasonable. *Don't read into it. That's a culturally acceptable way to end a letter. It's like "best" or "take care." People sign off like that all the time. It doesn't mean anything. It's just a word!*

But his lizard brain didn't give a shit. His lizard brain rolled around in it like a dog in sunlight. Luxuriated in that single, loaded syllable.

Yours.

He felt the grin tugging at his face before he even noticed it. One of those dumb, involuntary, *fuck-I'm-smiling* smiles. He tried to fight it, to lock his mouth into neutral, but it was too late.

He folded the letter carefully. Held it for a second. Then tucked it into the back of The Great Gatsby, where he kept all the dangerous things now.

And of course, that's when Luis walked by. "Yo," Luis said, squinting at him. "What's with the face?"

James didn't answer right away.

Luis leaned in a little. "You got mail or something?"

James looked up, expression flat. The kind that said: *Fuck off. None of your business.*

Luis smirked. "That college girl again?"

James shrugged. "Just a scam," he said. And then, softer, "A long con."

But Luis didn't leave. Instead, he leaned over a little too casually, like he was just stretching his back or checking the time. And then he saw it. The small photo. Stuck in the pages of Chapter 5.

Luis froze. "Yo... is that her?"

James snapped the book shut, a little too fast. Too late.

Luis raised both eyebrows, then grinned–wide and wolfish. "*That's* your pen pal?"

James said nothing. Just slipped the book under his bunk like it was nothing.

Luis gave a low whistle. "Damn. *DAMN.*" He shook his head and exhaled. Then laughing, "And I thought for sure it was going to be a fat old man. A classic catfish. Like definitely a dude."

James stared straight ahead. "She is."

Luis turned to leave, chuckling almost to himself. "Nah, bro. I've seen catfish. That ain't catfish. That's not even in the same food group." He paused. Just long enough to make it stick. "That girl is REAL."

James didn't move. The words echoed louder when someone else said them. It was one thing to think it in the quiet, to imagine it in the dark. It was something else entirely to hear it spoken out loud. Like confirmation. Like exposure.

That girl is REAL.

He'd been hanging onto the idea that maybe this was a fantasy. A carefully calibrated performance algorithmically tailored to trap him. He was hoping, in the stupidest possible way, that this was all just a con. That someone out there had engineered the perfect bait just for him. Because if it was fake, then it would only break him. He would take the hit. He wouldn't have to drag Minjee/Greg/whoever down with him.

But now someone else had seen her. And said it outloud.

She wasn't Greg. She wasn't a clever trick. She was a girl in a black dress with an orange necklace and a laugh you could feel through a photo.

She was a letter that said *You. Yours.*

James leaned forward, elbows on his knees, head in his hands.

22.

Dear Minjee,

Why did you have to send me a picture? I could've kept believing you were that asshole Greg if you hadn't sent it. It's hard to look at, honestly. Because it just makes me want to hear you laugh.

So here's Life Five. Otherwise you'll send me another letter full of double entendres and perfect timing, and I'll wake up... bothered.

Trials are boring. Even when they're damning you to hell. Especially when they're walking the jury through every spreadsheet you ever built and mapping exactly how it moved shipments across state lines. So much paperwork. So many slides. And somehow, every one of them means you're going to prison.

I had a great lawyer. A platinum blonde Armenian. Sharp. Fierce. She went to war for me.

The prosecutor was this young Asian guy. Polished. Eager. Reminded me of someone I might've known in high school. Maybe someone I sat next to in AP Calc. Maybe someone who went to Williams.

He wasn't brilliant, but he didn't have to be. I'd given him everything-every number, every row, every transaction. All he had to do was show up, click through the evidence, and let my empire fall apart at the seams. No style, no finesse needed. Just the facts were enough to bury me.

But my lawyer got everyone at the table. And somehow, I got a plea deal. Minimum security. 18 months. Unheard of.

That was the win. And then I found out I was a dreamer. Not like, dreamy. Or hopeful. I mean undocumented.

I've never traveled outside the States. Never tried to get a passport. So I didn't know. But apparently, I'm not a U.S. citizen. I'm a citizen of the Republic of Korea. Technically.

So now I'm in Lompoc waiting for an immigration judge to decide whether I stay or get deported.

That's Life Five.

It's a long way down from trying to be the Chick-fil-A of party pills to sitting in a prison library, waiting to see if you belong anywhere.

I'm a failure in every possible way. And I've even failed at scaring you away.

So yeah. I really don't like that picture.

-James

Minjee pressed a hand to her chest, tenderly or perhaps just instinctively, as if her body needed to protect something suddenly too soft, too exposed.

She had thought she had already known his worst.

His mother's death. The prison time. The collapse of everything he'd once tried to build. She thought she knew the edges of his pain. That the falling had already happened, and that what she was witnessing now–through these carefully worded, slightly sarcastic letters–was just catching his breath somewhere at the bottom.

But it hadn't been the bottom. Not yet.

He was still falling. Still suspended in some impossible, unfinished space. Waiting for a judge, waiting for a verdict, waiting to find out whether the only country he had ever known would let him stay.

And she'd sent him a photo. Laughing. Full of life. Unaware.

She sat there, the letter still open in her lap–almost bruising, like something alive, like something that could bleed out if she folded it wrong.

Because now she understood: she hadn't been writing to a man recovering. She had been writing to a man mid-fall. And she'd only just realized there was farther left to go.

23.

Dear James,

If it's easier, just think of me as Greg. Now it's catfishing in reverse: a girl trying to convince you that she's actually a fat old man with too many house cats and a crypto wallet full of stolen dreams. (Note: if anyone here is a failure, it's me. As a scammer. I have $0 worth of Bitcoin from you so far. Frankly, it's embarrassing.)

Thank you for sharing Life Five with me. I felt that one in my chest-the ache, the limbo.

I wish I were an immigration lawyer. Or at least someone who could say something useful.

Your downfall-your epic downfall, as you once called it-was really just your own brand of excellence catching up to you. If you hadn't been so good at what you did, if you hadn't built such flawless systems, been so meticulous with the spreadsheets, so smart with the logistics, maybe you wouldn't have gotten taken down like that. The same precision that made everything work is what sealed your fate. On the way up, it was your engine. On the way down, it was your paper trail.

I don't know. Maybe that's all of us. Our best parts are always the ones that undo us, eventually.

Does it work in reverse? Do our worst parts ever have the power to redeem us? My worst part is that I still don't really know who I'm supposed to be. Some days I think I can save the world. Other days I just wish I didn't feel so ashamed *that I can't speak Korean. Could that somehow become my best part? I'm not sure how that can be true but maybe I'll think about that for a while.*

Anyway.

How about I bake you a chess pie? With a nail file in it. So you can <u>Shawshank Redemption</u> your way out.

(For the record: Chess pie is awesome. It's sugar, butter, and eggs. That's it. It is the whitest dessert in the game but it's also southern. Which means, it's probably Black. Please show some respect.)

Also, can we just pause on this one detail? This whole time I thought I was writing to a Korean-American guy... But it turns out I've been writing to a Korean. Like an official, stamped-by-the-Republic, can-legally-judge-my-pronunciation Korean. You can officially validate my kimchi card now.

When do you hear back from the judge?

Yours,

Greg

James mopped the last streak of half-dried vomit off the linoleum and squeezed it out in the bucket. Dinner had been over for an hour, but a vague smell still lingered: a mix of industrial chili, bleach, and a sourness that off-brand Pine Sol couldn't quite kill.

He was alone in the cafeteria. Mendez, the guard on shift, just left him to it these days. No hovering. No checking in. James cleaned up, didn't cause problems. There was an understanding. So he tossed the mop with the others, propped like limp soldiers in the corner. The overhead lights hummed. Someone had carved a penis into the table in front of him.

It was as peaceful as this place got. And he'd been saving it. For this.

Her letter.

He unfolded it carefully, smoothing the creases with calloused fingers. Set it next to the chipped mug of coffee. It was the kind of coffee that had given up on being good but was still trying to be useful. At least warming. It was ritual.

Sometimes she dashed off a letter on perforated notebook paper or thin, elegant stationery. But this was on thicker linen stock. With a gel pen. He wanted a moment with it.

He read it again, slower this time. The idea of her reverse catfishing. He smirked. That bit about her having zero dollars of his crypto? He huffed out a laugh before he could stop it. Then he got to the part about his downfall. Her calling it his "*brand of excellence*" catching up to him.

He sat back in the cafeteria chair and exhaled through his nose.

James considered how she saw him. Not as some dumbass who flew too close to the sun. But as someone whose precision, whose design, was his undoing. Like he engineered the guillotine that eventually took his own head. No one had ever said it that way before.

He closed his eyes.

He would've liked arguing with her in a too-hot kitchen. Would've liked teasing her for the chess pie, and then devouring half of it. Would've liked listening to her worry about not speaking Korean while pretending not to notice the shape of her mouth.

He shook it off. He couldn't go there. Shouldn't.

He wasn't the guy who got invited home to Nashville. He wasn't the guy who met the parents, or sat cross-legged on a couch holding a mug of tea. He was the guy who got too good at moving pills across state lines. The guy who trained shapely women to deliver MDMA like Girl Scout cookies. The guy whose only current address was a federal facility, who might not even belong in the country he grew up in.

But still. She said she wanted to bake him a pie.

And somehow that image–the phantom warmth of a kitchen he'd never see and a mysterious dessert he'd never taste–wrapped around him. Not like a fantasy. Not like lust. But like comfort. Like someone saw shivering and thought to bring a blanket.

Shit. This was *dangerous.* Her voice, her wit, the way she folded humor around ache like pastry dough–it was going to kill him. Quietly. Softly. Without ever meaning to.

He folded the letter back up. Sipped the coffee, now lukewarm.

Then he went back to work. But he couldn't help but think it again. Minjee thought he was worth a pie.

24.

Dear "Greg",

You're right. It's easier if I think of you as fat Greg. (Also, your crypto scam is extremely low-yield. Don't quit slicing those rat brains.)

First-thank you.

That's not a thing I say often, or easily. But thank you for the way you saw me. Not as the sum total of my rap sheet, or some cautionary tale, but as someone who was very good at building something very wrong. I used to take pride in that kind of excellence. Still do, maybe. And that's a hard thing to admit, especially knowing where I ended up.

Second-the worst of us.

You asked if our worst parts could redeem us. Maybe your shame around not speaking Korean is your worst part. But from where I'm sitting, it's the part that's made you curious. Self-aware. Humble even though you also think you can change the world. Awake in ways most people aren't. That doesn't sound like a flaw to me. Frodo didn't speak a lick of Korean either, but it was his doubt that allowed him to carry the ring.

Maybe not knowing is the gift. Maybe if you'd grown up fluent, you wouldn't have needed to search. Maybe you wouldn't have found your way to letters. To strangers. To me.

Same goes for me. I wouldn't have written to someone like you if I weren't here. I don't think we would have ever *"met". I would've kept moving. Kept building. Kept winning at the wrong game. Prison is a lot of things, most of them bad, but it's also the only way I would've slowed down enough to really see someone. Or be seen. Even if it's by a possible crypto scammer with a fake Southern accent and a suspicious interest in baking.*

Speaking of which: Are you a real Southern girl? Like, were you a debutante that went to cotillions? Do you own pearls? Or was it more Waffle House and wearing overalls while smoking? Should I be worried that you have strong opinions about hot chicken?

Also, I need more context about the rat brains. Do you actually enjoy slicing them up or is it just something you tolerate while low-key mourning your pre-med dreams? What made you give that up? Maybe you could still become a solid brain surgeon, if only for the chance to drop literary references while cracking open skulls.

Still skeptical about this "chess pie." Sounds made up. But fine, I'll allow it. Just don't start talking about Jell-O salad or we're done.

–James

Minjee was walking slow, taking her time up Westwood Boulevard. It was late afternoon, the kind where the breeze was just warm enough to feel like permission. Students passed her, headphones on, backpacks slung low. She let them flow around her, not in a hurry to be anywhere. The letter was in her bag, already folded and re-folded and tucked away safely.

She'd read it three times. Wasn't even pretending not to smile anymore.

"Frodo didn't speak a lick of Korean either..."

She laughed–soft, breathy–like if she laughed louder, someone might hear her being seen. She loved Tolkien. Had for years. But she'd never seen herself in Frodo. Not really. He was brave. Loyal. Chosen. She'd always identified more with the ones who stayed in Hobbiton, cooking a second breakfast. Watching. Waiting.

She had never imagined that her not-knowing–her shame, her restless questioning–could be anything but a flaw. But now, here was this man, a stranger in a prison library she had never laid eyes on, calling it a gift.

Not to make her feel better. But like he just noticed it off-hand. Like the thing she most wanted to hide was the very thing that made her capable. Made her necessary. Like it was the reason she could carry something heavy. Something that mattered. Like doubt didn't disqualify her. It prepared her.

The breeze kicked up. She tucked a lock of hair behind her ear and kept walking. Her shadow stretched long ahead of her. She was thinking about James, about the way he saw things. Not just her, but the edges of her. The depths of her. The parts even she hadn't named yet.

And then, without meaning to, she was thinking about the dress. The white one. The Junior League cotillion. Austin, the son of her dad's golfing buddy, who had been her first kiss. Of course she owned pearls. Wore them to her cousin's wedding last spring. Smiled in the photos. Sat at the right table. Played the part.

She'd always tried to be good. Grateful. Easy to love.

Her parents were lovely. Truly. Quiet, gentle, generous people who never asked for more than she was willing to give. They adopted a Korean baby because they couldn't conceive, but believed in love. And they gave it. Unconditionally. But they never expected her to have questions she didn't know how to ask.

They didn't see the anger.

She closed her eyes and grimaced, for just a second. A flash.

Didn't see that some part of her–some irrational, infantile, persistent part–still burned at being left.

She'd always told herself the story the right way: it wasn't about her. It was economics. Stigma. Bad timing. But there was another story, the one she kept pressed down like a weed she couldn't kill: *Someone didn't want me. Not even as a baby. Not even then.*

This man, this stranger, was telling her that weakness didn't disqualify her. That she could still carry the ring. That she could because of the very worst part of her. That being left hadn't made her unworthy. It had made her ready.

And now here she was, walking toward campus, half-grateful to James for calling her Frodo, half-grappling with the fact that she'd never said any of this out loud. Not to her parents. Not to a friend.

More than that, she wanted to say these things to him. Some guy. Some man in a federal prison who didn't quite have a country. Who'd built something sharp and sleek and illegal, and watched it fall apart. Who wrote with restraint and steel and then, suddenly, softness. Who told her about his systems, his downfall, his mother, his best and his worst.

He'd told her more than most people say out loud in a lifetime. And he'd done it with a ballpoint pen. From behind a wall. And now he was in her head. In her thoughts. In her.

It was ridiculous. And it made perfect sense. Because somehow, in all that honesty–in the careful, steady reveal of his lives–he'd made her want to tell him things she hadn't told anyone. The things that didn't fit in polite conversation. The things that weren't sweet. Or grateful. Or easy to love.

She was only saying it to herself now because of a letter. Because of him.

So she kept walking. One foot in front of the other, wind at her back. Letter folded in her bag like it meant something. Which, clearly, it did.

25

Dear James,

Okay. First things first: I've enclosed a photo. You're welcome. It's Greg, aka Dennis Nedry from Jurassic Park, *behind a computer, checking on his Bitcoins. I need you to imagine him when you think of me.*

Also, is it Bitcoin or -coins? It has chains? Of... blocks? And you need a computer to see them? And you put them in a wallet? Where is said wallet? I cut up rat brains for a paycheck and this is well above my pay grade.

I've been thinking about what you said, about taking pride in the thing that brought you down. I don't have a neat reply, but I guess I hope you get to use that mind again. That you get to build something good with it. I'm not saying you built something evil, by the way. (You did, however, run a multi-city drug delivery empire with HR practices that—let's be honest—sound mildly illegal even without the drugs. So... a little judgment. But the affectionate kind.)

Yet, it was incredible what you built. What you learned. The way you saw how things could work and then made them work. I hope you get to do that again. Just with fewer felony implications.

And yes. Cotillion was real. White dresses, long gloves, lanky boys in tuxedos. My escort's name was Austin. We danced to a string quartet version of a Beyoncé song. There were feathers. And of course I own pearls. (Do you know people who don't? I don't believe it.)

I think I was helping my parents live out a version of my life that felt very Nashville. Like they were nudging me gently toward the Southern dream: Go to Vanderbilt. Join a sorority. Marry a boy with good manners and bad politics. Wear heels and pearls while I fry up chicken and serve grits to a man who calls me "darlin'" and mansplains credit cards like it's foreplay.

And honestly? I could have been good at it. Because I love to cook. Really cook. Give me a cast iron skillet, a stick of butter, and twenty minutes, and I'll make magic happen. On Saturdays I make brunch for my roommates, and Rosalie (my best friend, also writing to an inmate) swears I could charge for it.

Which brings me to Frodo. I imagined Frodo trying to speak Korean, and I laughed. Like, actual LOL, not just people texting that without making a sound. Did you know I loved Tolkien? Did you know what it would mean to me to be compared to Frodo? Not because I was brave or noble or chosen, but because of my flaws... my shame?

I've re-read those books at least three times. And I never saw myself in him. Until you did. You saw something I hadn't seen in myself.

I've spent my whole life trying to be easy to love. Good. Grateful. My parents chose me and that matters. They've loved me consistently without ever asking too much. And I've worked hard to protect them from the parts of me that feel broken. I've tried to be enough. Tried to make their choice worth it.

But the truth? I was abandoned.

You think I'm innocent. But the only time I was actually innocent-newborn, blank-slate, baby me-someone left me. In a church. Wrapped in a blanket. Left like a package delivered to the wrong address. And yes, I understand it was probably circumstance, shame, economics. I know it wasn't personal.

But it sure feels personal. Because someone saw me-tiny, helpless, alive-and still walked away. Didn't care if I lived or died.

And I've never said that before. Not to my parents. Not to friends. Not even in the sad journaling phase of high school. Because it makes me sound angry. And Cotillion girls aren't supposed to be angry. We're supposed to be sweet. Polished. Low-maintenance. We bake pies and smile in church and don't say what hurts.

But I am angry. And irrationally so. And somehow, you got me to say it. With only a pen. By comparing me to Frodo.

How did you do that?

Yours,

Minjee

P.S. I think my prom date only asked me out because he tried my strawberry Jell-O pretzel salad. Don't knock it.

James sat in the far corner of the library, tucked behind a cart of donated hardcovers that hadn't moved in weeks.

It was quiet. Quiet in the way only prisons get, suspiciously still, like even the air was being guarded. He was supposed to be shelving books, but he'd been sitting there for twenty minutes with the same open volume and her letter folded beside it like it was part of a table setting.

He'd spotted the book in passing. But after her last letter, he made a beeline for it: a community cookbook from Georgia complete with grainy photos and handwriting in the margins. He flipped to the desserts, found the pies, and started skimming.

Chess pie. Eggs. Sugar. Butter. Really? That was it?

He flipped again. *Jell-O pretzel salad.* Cool Whip. Cream cheese. Pretzels and gelatin in a dish that defied reason. Hers had strawberries.

His gaze lingered on the recipe. He pictured her, teenage Minjee, in a white dress and pearls, carrying that Jell-O monstrosity in a heavy, old-fashioned pie dish. He would've taken her to prom no matter what it tasted like.

Then another image came in. One she hadn't meant to describe. The baby on the church steps. Swaddled. Waiting. Chosen, eventually... but not at first.

He closed his eyes.

There was a part of him, deep and aching, that wanted to hold her. Not the girl with the pie plate and the pearls. The baby. The innocent. The one nobody stayed for. He didn't have words for that feeling. Just a sharp pull in his chest, strange and overwhelming. He wanted to wrap his arms around that version of her and whisper something useless like: *You're wanted. You're wanted. You're wanted.*

Then a door closed somewhere down the hall and his eyes burst open.

He flipped the book closed, resigned. "Don't be a dumbass," he exhaled.

This wasn't his life. These weren't his stories. He could touch her only in words, and even that was borrowed from Tolkien. She was out there making brunch and studying hippocampi, and for one fragile moment, she had written to him about anger and being left behind.

And he was a guy in a federal facility trying to imagine the taste of a pie he'd never eat, in a kitchen he'd never see.

He stared at the closed cookbook, something given away that he'd come looking for. He knew what it meant to be wanted in the wrong time, the wrong place. He knew what it meant to be wanted too late.

26.

Dear Frodo,

Thank you for the updated photo of Greg. A true specimen. I'll be sure to look at it fondly before going to sleep each night. I'm glad you finally fessed up and revealed the truth. Honesty's important especially if we're going to be friends.

Let's talk about this so-called "strawberry Jell-O pretzel salad." Four words. One dish. Not a vegetable in sight. But a key ingredient is Cool Whip. Which I believe does not legally count as a food but is a godless engineering marvel of humanity. I don't know whether to be confused or deeply impressed.

As for your cooking in general... Minjee. Come on.

Cast iron? Butter? Saturday brunch for your roommates? You do realize this is cruel and unusual punishment, right? You cannot just write things like that to a man in prison. I'm already at a disadvantage. Your letter had me imagining you in an apron and heels and pearls with flour on your cheek, and suddenly I need to stand up and pace the room for reasons I won't specify. It's-how do I say this politely?-more effective than the bra.

You said you could have lived that life, the one with Vanderbilt and the sorority and the man explaining APR to you in a husky voice. But you didn't. So I'm curious. How did you end up out west? What made you pack up your enchanted cast iron and head to UCLA?

Also, do you really want me to mansplain Bitcoin to you? Because I can. I bought ten dollars' worth back when it was about forty cents per coin. It was part of a half-baked plan to test whether it could work as an off-the-grid cash transfer system. I never got to scale the idea because... well, you know. Downfall, etc. But I still have the wallet. No idea what it's worth now. Probably enough to get a few bulk tubs of Cool Whip at Costco.

You're not hard to see, Minjee. At least not by me. I don't know if you try to hide in real life, but your letters say more than you think.

What you wrote about being abandoned, about the church, stayed with me. It's still here. Still pressing down on me. I don't know what it is to be left like that. You once said you didn't know what it's like to lose someone who had been fully there. I don't know how someone looked at you, so fully there, and walked away. I don't know how someone dropped you off in a world that wasn't excitedly waiting for you.

The only thing I can say: I'm glad you were found. And I'm sorry you had to wait.

Have you ever thought about looking? For the church, the paperwork, anything? Or even just going back, to see what Korea might mean to you now?

–James

Minjee flushed. Not in the caught-off-guard way she had earlier in their letters, like when she accidentally brought up bras. This time it was deeper. A slow, spreading warmth that crept up her neck and landed somewhere just behind her cheeks.

An Asian-American guy getting turned on by the most Southern version of her? The pearls, the cast iron, the flour on her cheek? It wasn't what she expected. Nashville boys had liked it when she seemed shy and slender. They didn't like it as much when she dropped a <u>Brave New World</u> reference right as they tried to slip a tongue in her mouth. But James? He was out here with what could only be described as a Southern fetish.

Greg hadn't been an amateur, apparently. Greg had seduced James without even trying. Just with butter and a preposterous "salad" that involved no actual greens. (Well, her version did have a mint garnish.)

But the flush, that deeper thing, came from the part of her that now wanted to cook for him. To fry up something messy and golden, slide it onto a sun-warmed porcelain plate, and watch him try not to lose his mind. To make him pace the room for reasons he wouldn't specify.

The bra had been obvious. This was different. It was slower. Stranger. Domestic. The kind of seduction that came from actually knowing someone. From being known in return.

Then she reread the paragraph about the church. The baby. Being fully there.

He had seen her. Not just the girl who writes letters and makes pie jokes. But her. The part she usually keeps under lock and Southern charm. And somehow, he didn't look away. He didn't pity her. He didn't fix it.

He just made her feel, for a second, like maybe someone had been waiting for her. Like the world hadn't quite given up on her being fully there. And fully here.

She wiped her nose with the back of her sleeve. No tears. Just a sniffle. There was a hum. Or was it a sting? At any rate, something small and steady.

She sat with it for a moment. Then pulled her laptop into her lap. Typed "bitcoin price" into the search bar and smiled.

27.

Dear James,

You're relieved I finally sent an accurate photo! Greg's put on a little weight since then, but he still wants you to think he's pretty. Even if he's not as pretty as your club girls.

Let's talk about this "off-the-grid cash transfer system" you almost invented. Ten dollars at forty cents a coin? I did a little digging. Bitcoin is now worth... drumroll please... almost five bucks a coin! Congratulations, you're a hundredaire. Greg is thrilled that his scam might finally pay off.

Now stick'em up! Gimme... your wallet password? Your Bitcoin transfer code? Is it a blockchain login? Whatever it is that unlocks the moola. At the risk of you losing your brand new $125 fortune, can you please explain how a wallet manages a chain of blocks that somehow becomes real money? (And if you explain it well enough, you will once again be the mastermind of your own downfall. Greg believes in you.)

Also, the fact you're even a little hot and bothered by the apron fantasy says more about you than it does about me. Don't you regret making fun of my chess pie now? And because of that great sin, may you never, ever touch my brown butter cornbread. It's sacred. It's the reason I lug my well-seasoned cast iron pan from apartment to apartment like it's part of my personality. Rosalie says it could get me married if I wanted. So congratulations. You've been banned from the good stuff. Unless, of course, you find a way to redeem yourself.

I've been trying to learn how to cook Korean food. My amazing non-Korean roommates introduced me to H Mart, which is basically a magical wonderland of ingredients I've never seen before. I spend forever there, just walking up and down the aisles, trying to match what I see in the Korean cookbooks to what's on the shelves.

So far I've made japchae and mandoo. I follow the recipes exactly, but I still don't really know how it's supposed to taste. I have a feeling I'm making Southern versions of both. Like, japchae that Dolly Parton might like or mandoo with an Elvis sneer. I might try pan-frying the next batch in a little lard, just to see what happens.

And I finally get why my Asian friends roll their eyes at "Southern dumplings." After eating pan-fried mandoo and xiao long bao, I officially rescind my previous dumpling claims. I now refer to Southern dumplings as: delicious homey dough balls in gravy. More accurate. Still yummy.

And just... thank you.

For seeing me.

For not flinching.

For not trying to fix it.

For just letting it be.

For letting me be... not quite rational.

And yes, I've thought about going back to Korea. I don't know what I'd be looking for exactly. Documents? Buildings? Stories? Maybe just proof that I came from somewhere real. I don't know if I'll ever do it. I don't know how *my parents would feel. I don't want them to think they weren't enough. But yeah, I think about it.*

As for how I ended up out west... that's a longer story. I'll tell you if you tell me something about Life Six. The one currently in progress. The life after the fall. The one that isn't fully written yet.

Yours,
Minjee

James stared at the folded letter, shaking his head. A man could only take so much.

He considered writing back with a punishing string of double entendres. Just to even the score.

So I can't touch your cornbread, huh? Well, I think the cornbread might be ready. Slick with butter. Hot.

And your cast iron might need a little oil and friction to feel good.

You had me at "delicious homey dough balls in gravy."

He imagined the words on paper and then chuckled, wiping them away in his head like steam off a mirror. *Nope.* That definitely wasn't going to help with the pacing. No siree.

He shook his head, smiling despite himself.

"I want it. Bad."

That line still woke him up sometimes.

He heard footsteps before he saw Luis.

"Yo," Luis said, tapping the letter with his finger. "You get another one?"

James didn't answer.

Luis tilted his head. "You gonna tell her to visit?"

James snorted. "It's like a three-hour drive from LA. She's not coming to Lompoc. She's a rat neuroscientist or something. You think those rats feed themselves?"

Luis raised an eyebrow. "So you're saying there's a chance."

James didn't respond.

"You're not the least bit curious?" Luis pressed.

James slid the letter behind his head and laid back on his bunk. "I don't need to be curious," he said. "I already know how it ends."

But he didn't sound like he meant it. Not even to himself.

28.

Dear Greg,

First of all: you are better than pretty. You're beautiful, sure. But you're also something else entirely. You're someone I'd give my Bitcoin to.

It's the way you laugh. Like you're full of life and the rest of us forgot how to breathe. Like the air you take in is different. Lighter. Fresher. It's unfair, honestly, to those poor club girls. They never stood a chance against you... Greg.

Now, I suppose it's time for a formal apology. From the depths of my soul. For my past comments regarding chess pie. I didn't know what I was saying. I was young and I was foolish. Please allow me the opportunity to earn back your trust and, someday, touch your brown butter cornbread. (And for the record, you are the one making it sound like a double entendre. I'm just quoting you.)

Also, this is me formally acknowledging that your mandoo game might be more Korean than mine. I've never made it from scratch. I've eaten plenty, but always frozen or made by someone's mom. If you're actually making the filling and folding it by hand? That's advanced. If you're pan-frying it in lard? That's not just Korean. That's innovation. Korean 2.0.

I think food is one of the ways we are something; not just how we try to feel it. The way you talk about songpyun, or mandoo, or those godforsaken homey dough balls in gravy...

that's identity. That's belonging. Even if the recipes are half-wrong. Especially when they're improvised.

You don't have to become Korean. You already are. I'll just add your name to the VIP list.

Which brings me to the real reason for our entire correspondence: your ongoing effort to steal my $125 fortune.

Let's start here. The "wallet" is not made of leather and doesn't go in a purse. It's a digital private key, a long string of letters and numbers that gives you access to your Bitcoin. You don't get the password to the wallet. The wallet is the password.

Bitcoin is built on the blockchain, basically a giant communal spreadsheet where everyone has a copy. Every transaction (i.e., every line of the spreadsheet) is verified and locked in by a bunch of computers solving math problems. Which makes it incredibly secure and also incredibly stupid. Your wallet lets you see which of those transactions, which bits of imaginary internet gold, belong to you.

When I "invested" my measly $10, I thought it might be useful for transferring cash between franchisees. Maybe it could've worked. But eventually someone would've figured out how to trace the transactions buried under all that math. I've accepted that spreadsheets and ledgers, of any kind, will always lead to my downfall.

All that to say, if you want to steal my Bitcoin, you'll have to get me to tell you my private wallet key. Good luck, Greg!

And as for you Minjee, what are you doing? "Stick 'em up"? You sound like you're holding up a Wells Fargo stage-

coach while wearing a bandana, spittin' into a tin cup. You are not Jesse James.

Consider this: If the Artful Dodger had your resources, he'd charm the pants off me and initiate a wallet transfer before I realized the heist had already happened. Use your feminine wiles. Feign a small but emotionally manipulative tragedy that requires exactly $125. Or offer a suggestive photo (tasteful, of course) in exchange for the key. Come on, Minjee. You're a clever girl with a bright future in fraud. Don't waste your potential.

You wrote something I keep coming back to, that you were "not quite rational." But sometimes the irrational thing is what cracks the surface. Gets us to combine pretzels and gelatin. Or write a letter to a stranger in prison. Or go look for a church in Korea with a memory buried in the walls.

You asked about Life Six. The part I'm living now. There were a few months where I stared at walls and tried not to go under. But mostly, it's marked by these letters. That's the water I swim in these days.

What are you doing this summer?

Just curious.

–James

She laughed. "Touch your brown butter cornbread," she said to the empty room, and immediately cracked up at how much worse it sounded now.

She hadn't meant for that phrase to stick. But there it was, lodged in her brain forever, somewhere between the memory of the first time she felt a boy's erection through his jeans and the day she accidentally discovered her roommate's vibrator.

She pressed her fingers to her mouth, grinning.

He wants to touch the cornbread, she thought. *Because he likes the way Greg laughs.*

She said it to herself as a joke. Kind of.

But then she pictured him. Not clearly. Just the vague outline of a man, sitting somewhere cold and fluorescent, holding the photo she'd sent. Staring at it. At her. At the laugh she hadn't staged, hadn't planned.

The thought knocked something loose.

And then, like a wave, came heat. An ache. A sudden, baffling need to see him. Not the letters. Not the voice she imagined in his sentences. *Him.*

She reached for her laptop without thinking. Opened a new tab. Typed "Lompoc federal prison."

Map. Images. Driving directions.

It was... not that far. An hour from Santa Barbara.

She blinked. That felt uncomfortably close. Like possibility.

Rosalie was doing that kids' science camp at UCSB. She had applied too. Summer money. They could be roommates.

And UCSB had a few behavioral neuroscience research labs. Her PI had a collaborator there. A woman Minjee had quietly admired from afar. She could... ask. Send an email. Just to see.

She closed the laptop and sat still for a second. It wasn't a plan. Not really.

What would happen to this if they met? Wculd the spell be broken? What if he wasn't what she thought he was? What *was* he? What was *this*?

29.

He got the letter a little sooner than expected. Not by much. A day or two, maybe. Enough to notice. Enough to be surprised.

He figured it was just a quick reply. He didn't sit down. Didn't wait. Just tore it open at the edge of the corridor on his way to the library, still half-thinking about something else.

He didn't read it. Not as sentences, not as words. He *saw* it. Three lines. Four, if you counted the name.

Dear James,
Could I visit you?
Yours,
Minjee

He stopped walking. Just stood there. He stared at the page like it might rearrange itself into something that would make more sense. Like maybe, if he blinked hard, the words would flicker and mean something else.

The hallway buzzed behind him but it all went quiet in his head.

"Could I visit you?"

His breath caught, low and tight in his chest. Had he somehow willed this into being? Was this the thing he wanted so badly it tricked the universe into saying yes?

He thought back through his letters. He didn't ask her, right? He wanted to. God, he almost did. So many times. But he didn't. Right?

He flipped the page over. Checked the back. Maybe he'd find a "JK sucker" in Luis's handwriting.

But it was just lines. Just her notebook paper.

And suddenly, then the floor beneath him didn't feel quite the same.

Part 3

Seoul

Present Day

Dohee slipped off her sneakers and stepped inside, the part-Chihuahua, part-Yorkie, all-yappy dog squirming in her arms. The apartment was warm, the windows cracked just enough to let in the early evening air. She heard the soft clink of chopsticks and the rustle of workbook pages before she saw him.

Dohyun was kneeling at the low table, bent over a stack of worksheets, his bare feet hooked under him, a pencil in his mouth. He looked up as she came in and immediately abandoned everything.

"Frodo!" he shouted, jumping up and scrambling across the floor to throw his arms around the dog.

Dohee sighed. "Dohyun, do not give this dog a reward for running off. He escaped. Again."

Frodo yapped once and licked her brother's cheek triumphantly. Dohyun giggled like it was the greatest moment of his day.

Dohee rolled her eyes but couldn't help smiling as she headed toward the kitchen.

Her mother didn't look up. She was standing at the stove, sleeves rolled, hair pinned back with a clip that had started to slip. The steam from the pot curled up in soft, fluffy waves.

"There's *boricha* (barley tea) in the fridge," her mother said.

"I know," Dohee said, already opening the door.

"Did you finish your *hagwon* (cram school) homework?"

Dohee hesitated. "I'm going to."

Her mother gave her a look. Not angry. Just disappointed and expectant, the way only moms could be.

"You have *suneung* (College Scholastic Ability Test) in a few months. No falling behind."

"I'm not behind."

"You're not ahead."

Dohee poured herself some barley tea and leaned casually toward the stove, peeking into the bubbling pot.

Dakdoritang. Red, glossy, simmering hard. Spicy chicken, carrots, and potatoes with that slightly sweet heat.

And then she saw it. On the counter, off to the side, cooling on the rack. Perfectly set. Slightly golden. A little cracked in the middle.

She didn't say anything. Just took a slow, cooling sip of tea.

Lompoc/Los Angeles - 2012

30.

Dear Minjee,

Do you really want to visit? Lompoc is a long way from Westwood.

And visitation to a federal facility is not straightforward. You'll need to fill out a form. There's a background check. You'll have to list your relationship to me (would it be strange to call us "friends"?). Approval takes a few weeks, and that's before we get into scheduling.

You won't be allowed to bring your phone or bag. You'll lock them up at the gate.

You'll sit across from me at a plastic table, possibly metal, always ugly. A correctional officer will be posted nearby, pretending not to listen. We'll get an hour, maybe two. You can hug me when you arrive and again when you leave. That's the extent of the physical contact allowed.

Laying it all out like this, it probably sounds like I'm trying to talk you out of it. I'm not. I hate that this letter might convince you not to come. But I need you to know what's actually involved. And you may decide it's not worth it. That's okay.

You're already here. In your letters. Between the margins. In the spaces between sentences.

If I've successfully discouraged you, that would be very on brand. You once said I was taken down by my own brand of excellence. This would fall into the same category.

Then again, maybe this is just the next phase of the scam. Classic Greg! Build trust. Establish emotional vulnerability. And just when the mark starts to feel safe, offer to show up in person.

It's brilliant, really. The con has immaculate pacing. He's upping the ante. At this point, there's almost nothing Greg couldn't get from me. Bank routing numbers. Credit card statements. My mother's maiden name. If the promise is the live, in-person arrival of a beautiful, brilliant girl who seems suspiciously tailored to get past all my usual defenses... Well, I'd probably hand it all over. I respect the craft.

I've included the form. You don't have to fill it out. You don't have to show up. The letters are enough.

I'd like that though. To see you.

–James

They were halfway back from H Mart when Rosalie asked, "So. Is Emily taking her rice cooker home for the summer, or are we going to borrow it for Santa Barbara?"

Minjee blinked, pulled out of her window-staring trance. "What?"

"For Santa Barbara," Rosalie repeated. "I'm not making rice in a pot like some unfortunate peasant now that we've lived in an apartment with a Zojirushi. I need to know."

"Emily said we can borrow it, as long as we're back by September," Minjee said.

Rosalie nodded, then glanced at her sideways. "So, I'm super thrilled we're both going to be counselors at Camp Sci Revolution, but... was this always the plan? Or did a certain federal inmate gently nudge you in this direction?"

Minjee hesitated. "I was going to apply either way."

"You had already applied, I remember. But..." Rosalie let the word hang.

Minjee pulled her legs up onto the seat, knees pressed to the dashboard. "It wasn't because of him. I didn't do it because of him. At least I don't think so. But..." She groaned. "I hate that I'm having to admit this. But I have an irrational desire to see him. To see what this is. To see if he's real."

Rosalie glanced over again, softer this time. "I don't think you're irrational. Just because this is weird doesn't mean it's irrational."

Minjee turned back to the window. "Am I crazy? Did he somehow con me? Is this emotional manipulation in the slowest, most literate form?"

Rosalie was quiet for a moment. "I've read the letters. Or okay, some of them. And heard about all of them. Repeatedly."

Minjee smiled, just barely.

"He's not sappy," Rosalie went on. "He's not asking for anything. He tells you not to come. He makes fun of your delicious desserts because he's an idiot. He calls you Greg. None of this is giving off 'master manipulator' energy."

Minjee exhaled. "But what if I'm reading him wrong? What if I meet him and it's... nothing?"

"Then you're in Santa Barbara," Rosalie said simply. "Having a great summer with me and the cute science campers and slicing a whole different set of rat brains and not writing letters anymore. Might as well find out."

There was a part of her that twinged at that. Not writing letters anymore.

Minjee nodded, her voice steadier than she felt. "You're right. I need to find out. And if it's bad, then that's helpful to me." She paused, then added, more to herself than to Rosalie, "I can quit while I'm ahead."

"But," Rosalie said, thinking out loud, "what if it's not nothing? What if it's good?"

Minjee blinked. That possibility scared her more than the other.

She said, "That might be worse."

They pulled up to a red light and turned down the little street toward their apartment. Rosalie picked up the parking garage opener and aimed it at the sensor.

"When we get home," she said, "show me the one he just sent."

Minjee nodded. She didn't say it out loud, but she already knew which line she'd reread again later.

"I'd like that though. To see you."

31.

Dear James,

You think forms scare me?

I belong to an extremely bureaucratic institution run by the state of California that considers me a nine-digit number. I've filled out forms that required me to calculate my parents' adjusted gross income from two years ago. I've filled out forms with questions like "Have you or a loved one been impacted by the 2007 subprime mortgage crisis?"

I am the queen of forms.

I would fill out your visitation form even if it had nothing to do with seeing you. Just to keep my skills sharp. Just for fun. So no, the paperwork doesn't scare me.

What does give me pause is that I still don't own $125 worth of Bitcoin. (Still haven't figured out how to set up a wallet. Apparently bitcoin.com doesn't just do that for you.) So I'm not entirely sure who's scamming whom here.

Have you considered that you might be the con? Don't inmates write to girls just to get them to visit? Maybe you're telling me exactly what I want to hear. Maybe you know that saying "You don't have to visit, the letters are enough" is precisely the kind of thing that would convince someone this isn't a con. In which case, well played.

But I also want you to know–it's not all about you. I'll be in Santa Barbara working as a camp counselor for a middle school science camp at UCSB. It's chaotic and funny and full of extremely small tweens in oversized goggles. The coun-

selors all pick nicknames for the summer, and no one uses their real names. I'm thinking of going by "Greg." It'll be like method acting.

Also, a UCSB professor, Dr. Camille Ramirez (think of her as queen of the hippocampus slices), said she'd be willing to take me on for a research project. It's not a funded position or anything, but she said she could use someone with a lot of experience slicing rat brains. So I was like: wow, thank you for seeing the true me. And no, that's not sarcasm. I'm genuinely thrilled! Ugh, this paragraph is starting to sound sarcastic, but I swear it's not. Please imagine me writing this with wide, unblinking eyes and a scalpel in hand. But not in a psychotic way.

Okay, maybe sarcasm is the safer option.

You asked me why I do it: The brain slicing. Oddly, it started with a sort of weird stats course–CourseKata. It used all this new-fangled stuff like programming in R and Jupyter notebooks, and somehow convinced me that I might actually be able to analyze data. Like, for real projects.

So I found a lab that needed my computational chops. Stuck around. Learned wet lab stuff. I told myself it looked good on a CV. Maybe med school someday. Maybe not.

But the truth is, I like getting lost in it. The precise, repetitive churn of lab work toward some tiny, specific goal. No one in the world really cares whether it's the hippocampus or the striatum that's responsible for spatial memory encoding. But we do.

We care. We obsess. For months. For a year. We chase the answer, re-run our code, make a million visualizations to see our data in different ways, and then we try to explain it to the world in a 60-slide PowerPoint no one asked for and a paper three people might read. It's strangely comforting. Like an achievable dream.

And yes, of course, I put "friend" on the form. What did you think I was going to write? Probable catfish? Unnamed emotional entanglement? Are you trying to DTR via federal paperwork?

In some ways, that's why I think we should meet. Not to define it. Just to see. What this is.

Yours,
Minjee

James sat outside his counselor's office, back against the cinderblock wall, the form folded in thirds and tucked in the front cover of <u>The Great Gatsby</u>.

The irony didn't escape him.

He'd known guys who ran the playbook: write to several girls on the outside, sweet-talk them into phone time, commissary, maybe a sexy picture or two. Make her feel like she was the only one. Make it easy to forget that she wasn't.

And yeah, he'd thought about it. Early on. Wondered if this would become some version of that.

But he chose a different path. That's why no one saw her photo. Not the usual trading-circle bullshit. Not passed around for commentary or laughs. Luis had seen it once, because Luis was a nosy bastard. Briefly.

It wasn't even a sexy photo. Or at least, not a nude one. Whether it was sexy was another question. Probably. But that wasn't the point. There was something inescapable about it.

In truth, James had slept with a fair number of beautiful, "sexy" women. And he remembered being vaguely annoyed by a thousand different parts of that experience. Waking up beside someone and not knowing her name. Wanting her gone so he could get on with the day. And being annoyed that he'd wasted the night.

He remembered there being good nights, too. Nights that felt easy, nice, even fun. But he couldn't recall a single one in detail. They'd all blurred together. Like trying to remember a specific drop of water in the middle of a shower. There was heat. Motion. Familiar rhythms. But nothing you could hold onto.

And underneath it all, a kind of static. Doubt. Insecurity. That low, constant discomfort. Never knowing if he was misreading the moment or she was. Not knowing whether he was rejecting or projecting. So much left unsaid. Always unsaid.

But her letters were different. All the doubt, all the insecurity, all the discomfort were there, but laid bare in sentences. Held steady in paragraphs. Written down. In pen. In cursive.

Her letters were so memorably her. He could recall specific lines. Specific moods. The times she signed as Minjee. The times she signed as Greg. The first time she signed *Yours*. One letter where the *y* in *yours* was almost lowercase. Another where the comma looked like a period. He remembered that.

He had never slept with her. Never touched her. Never even verified that she was the actual person behind the letters. But her picture reminded him of everything he remembered about her.

She didn't belong in this world. Which is why he kept the photo and her letters tucked inside <u>The Great Gatsby.</u> No one here gave a shit about Gatsby. Her photo lived quietly between the pages of Chapter 5. Right where Gatsby sees Daisy again.

James shifted slightly, felt the edge of the form press through the cover.

This was the part where guys usually got excited: when the mark took the bait and said she'd visit. That was the end game. Get the girl here. Get her to bring things. Do things.

But he felt... not panic, exactly. Just something tight in his chest. He didn't want to lose the letters. He didn't want to lose whatever this was before he understood it.

He knew the letter thing couldn't last forever. But meeting might throw cold water on it. Meeting him, in a place like this, might kill the image of Holden Caulfield with the fake IDs she'd been writing to.

Even so, he didn't even have to think twice about submitting the form.

Because if she was really coming–if somehow Greg had upgraded from mail fraud to in-person burglary, sending a hired girl to yell "Stick 'em up!" at him–he needed to see what that meant. He needed to see the girl who laughed. He needed to see what this was.

Minjee wanted to see it too.

He leaned his head back against the wall. Waited for his name to be called.

32.

Dear Minjee,

Sorry, I didn't realize you were the Queen of Forms. Truly. My mistake. I've been known to underestimate you before (see chess pie). I paid for that one. If I insult your bureaucratic prowess, I assume I'll be barred from ever tasting your delicious homey dough balls. (Again, let the record show, <u>you</u> are the one making these phrases sound suggestive, not me.)

Just so you're aware: the background check is real. I turned in the form, so now the feds have your full name, date of birth, and access to whatever criminal empire Greg's been running from behind that cat-food-Bitcoin-girl-offering-to-visit smokescreen. You good with that?

By the way, congratulations on getting to slice more rat brains. (That's a sincere sentence. I didn't think it ever could be, and yet here we are.) Is that your new path? Carefully answering wildly specific scientific questions and presenting them in 60-slide decks to grad students who are only there for the free cookies? If so, I admire it. I really do.

Also, you learned to program at UCLA? This whole "I can't figure out Bitcoin" now seems like misdirection from a very skilled hacker.

(To continue being your pen pal, should I know what a striatum is? My ganglion cells would like to see that explanation.)

And maybe I missed this somewhere: Did you graduate? Are congratulations in order? Are you now in that liminal post-grad summer where time is fake and your day job is still technically "student"? What's in store for Minjee after UCLA, armed with a neuroscience degree in one hand and her enchanted cast iron pan in the other?

If you think these letters are a con, that says more about you than it does about me. Which is to say, you might be a little strange. Because if you're reading these and thinking, "Wow, you're saying all the right things to me..."–well, I'm partly flattered. But mostly alarmed. How could I be saying all the right things when I've clearly spent a few lifetimes on wrong moves? You might be overestimating my emotional intelligence based on my handwriting. Or imagining me as someone I'm not. I guess I'm just hoping you are not too disappointed if you ever do meet me in person.

I know we already DTR-ed via federal paperwork as "friends," but I'll admit, it also feels strange to call us that. We don't have each other's phone numbers. You don't know what my face looks like. I don't know if you even know how to type. Or if you put hot sauce on your tacos. Or if you struggle to parallel park. So it sort of feels like we're not even friends.

And I've never wanted to meet a friend and not meet them at the same time.

Maybe we can chalk it up to these letters. They're better than anything I could've imagined. And sometimes, when things are good, you don't want to ask what they are. You just want them to keep going.

But if you're not scared off, and if you pass the background check, and if the person behind the letters actually shows up... then what?
–James

Minjee told herself she wouldn't reread it until she finished her paper. Just one more pass through the conclusion. One more paragraph where she managed to say "hippocampal map" three times without sounding demented. Just a little more focus.

She looked over. The letter was sitting exactly where she'd left it. Tucked back into the envelope. Tucked under her phone on the kitchen table. Like it had reluctantly agreed to wait.

The laundry basket was overflowing. The H Mart bags were still half-unpacked. A stack of flattened cardboard boxes leaned against the hallway wall, impatiently judging her.

She still needed to clear her side of the bedroom, pack everything that was hers, wipe down the fridge, figure out which pantry items to leave behind and which they'd take to Santa Barbara.

Emily's younger sister and her dorm friends were all moving in this weekend. The sublet was set. All the paperwork finalized, summer rent calculated to the decimal. All she had to do was turn in the damn paper, finish packing, and not emotionally combust.

But all she wanted to do–more than nap, more than watch YouTube, more than reward herself with a chai latte–was reread the latest letter from James.

Then reread the one before that.

And the one before that.

She hated that. Not in a real way. But in the way you hate things that make you feel too much.

She hated how much she looked forward to the letters. How they made her feel like space could really bend. Like she wasn't here and he wasn't there. Like they were meeting in a different dimension where there wasn't packing, or background checks. Somewhere he could taste her dough balls.

She smirked and shook her head. *Ugh, of course.* The way he played her words back at her. Infuriating. Hilarious. Magnetic.

He was right. They weren't friends. Not exactly. Only in the eyes of the federal government of the United States of America. She didn't know what they were. But she kept writing. And he kept writing back.

She stared at the envelope for a second longer, then dragged her laptop closer and forced herself to type another sentence about synaptic plasticity. When the cursor blinked at the end of it, she looked up.

Ten more minutes, she promised herself. Then she'd open it again. Just ten.

Dear James,

I don't usually speak in double entendres. I swear I have actually called chicken and dumplings "chicken and delicious homey dough balls." But now, thanks to you, I can't say it out loud without feeling like I'm making an inappropriate joke about my sweet grandmother's recipe, the one she taught me to make when I was nine. I may have to retire the dish altogether. Your fault.

Also, no, I didn't graduate this quarter. I have one more left. I started UCLA late and I still need two more classes to complete my major. And I want to stay and take this Asian-American history course.

My parents were a little surprised that I'm not doing the whole graduation spectacle with the rest of my friends. I think there was a way to petition to walk across the stage, but even if I were eligible, I don't think I'd want to. I'd rather spend the day learning to play racquetball, taking a spin in a classic low-rider, or picnicking in front of <u>Hamlet</u> in Griffith Park. Not taking photos. Not wearing leis. Not sweating through polyester robes.

All my life I've done things that were mostly for show. Cotillion, for example, really puts the "pomp" in pomp and circumstance. The ritual. The tradition. (Cue <u>Fiddler on the Roof</u> soundtrack.) But I don't think I want my time at UCLA to end that way.

It's part of why I came out west. (You make it sound like I was a pioneer with nothing but a cast iron pan rattling around in my covered wagon. In truth, I flew United and my parents picked up a rental car at the airport. So what I'm saying is: my life is very hard.)

If I'd gone to Vanderbilt, my life would've been about their rituals. Their traditions. Their timeline. They didn't even know I applied to UCLA. So it was a bit of a shock when I announced I was going here, even if that meant starting on the waitlist. My parents aren't the kind of people who get angry. But it was the closest thing to a fight we've ever had: a civil, slightly cold disagreement that lasted 5.5 days.

What they didn't know was the other reason I had wanted to be here. The adoption agency they used is based in LA. Seventeen-year-old me had a cockamamie plan to come here and find something. Someone. I don't even know. I just wanted to go somewhere that felt like it might still have a door.

Anyway.

About the possibility that you are conning me through these letters. Isn't that a thing prison guys do? Try to trap some clueless lady into sending particular kinds of photos? (I won't describe them. I learned my lesson since the b-r-a incident. You told me not to evoke that kind of thing. I'm trying to be good.) And I guess it's kind of a low bar that you've cleared: that you don't do that.

But it's also not that you're saying all the right things. Honestly, you say a lot of weird things. It's the unexpectedness that keeps me coming back.

I could've never anticipated how much low-level crime you committed during your Age of Innocence. I didn't know how Life Two could hold so much scrappiness and grief. Your Life Three continues to defy logic... and possibly HR regulations. There's something strange and deep about what you chose to call your "glory days," that quiet, disciplined stretch that ultimately brought you down. And the fall? I'm still reeling over the implications. I'm not sure I've fully processed it so I can't imagine what it's been like for you.

Every letter reveals something I wouldn't have predicted. And in all the words, in all the details, in all the stories–good or bad, little or big–you haven't disappointed me yet.

And maybe, if we meet and it's a total dud, we can just go into separate rooms and pass each other notes until the magic comes back.

By the way, of course I put hot sauce on my tacos (I'm not a psychopath). And I don't know if I struggle to parallel park because I've only really driven in Nashville. I typically avoid any situation where parallel parking might be required. I suspect I'd be atrocious at driving in LA. So... yes. Probably.

Yours,

Minjee

P.S. I'm glad I typed this letter out. Not just because it proves I can type. But because, hot damn, it's long!

Standing in front of the mailroom, James peeled open the envelope slowly, carefully, like it might tear if he didn't treat it right. It was two pages of 8x11 plain white copy paper. In some classy sans serif font like Helvetica.

Typed.

He stared at the pages for a second longer than necessary.

A letter from Minjee. But it was typed. It felt different. Not worse. Just... less embodied.

The words were still Minjee. Absolutely. The voice. The way she braided insight with mischief. The jokes she tossed over her shoulder, every one hitting its mark.

But he missed her handwriting. The way the y's looped long and narrow. The little cross-outs where she'd changed her mind mid-sentence. The moments where the ink got tighter, like she was cramming a thought into the margin instead of starting a new line.

She'd been on those pages. Her arms had held them down. Pressed her wrist to the corner while she thought. Pushed down with a pen to get a phrase just right. And now her touch was gone from the paper.

Still, the letter was long, longer than any she'd sent before. He stayed in her voice for what felt like hours. Read the whole thing, then went back and read the racquetball sentence twice, just because it made him smirk. He could see it: her in a low-rider, lazily cruising over the LA river.

She was staying. Taking another quarter. Not graduating yet. Not walking. He respected that. Even if he was slightly amused that her version of rebellion involved Hamlet in

Griffith Park and a possible course in Asian-American history.

He huffed out a laugh at the *b-r-a* line. As if spelling it with dashes would make it less erotic. As if the danger wasn't in the concept, but in the spacing of the letters.

Just then his counselor–an aging, bearded hipster named Sam with eagle eyes and a long memory–walked by and said, "That visit request you filed is moving along. Could be another two weeks though."

James nodded. Didn't ask for more. He rarely did.

Sam stopped, tucked a folder under his arm, and pushed his glasses up to his forehead. He gave James a quick glance. Not nosy, just observant, like always. "Relative?"

James hesitated. "Friend."

Sam looked at him for a beat longer. Not judging. Just noting something. Then he nodded once. "Hope you get to see your friend soon."

And that was it. No smile. No follow up. Just the kind of quiet acknowledgment James had come to expect from Sam, someone who didn't say much, but saw more than most.

James nodded again. "Yeah. Me too."

He didn't say: *She's not exactly my friend.* Didn't say: *She's the person whose handwriting I memorized before I knew her face.* Didn't say: *She's the girl I want to hear laugh.* He just went back to his bunk and opened the letter again.

Started reading it like it was the first time.

34.

Dear Minjee,

Okay. Fine. You know how to type. Your letter was long. Extremely long. You might have set a record for this correspondence.

The length... It was nice. It felt like you were here a little longer. Like we got to hang out without being interrupted.

I'll admit, you're a little different when you're represented by Helvetica (or Arial?). Your voice is still there but I missed the handwriting. The loops. The margins filled with sideways thoughts. The way some of the letters would run together, but I could still tell what you meant. There's something about knowing your palm pressed down on the page for a while. It felt like you were closer.

Still, Helvetica is better than nothing.

And now you're at a Santa Barbara address. I assume the mythical cast iron made the journey with you. If you were a Disney princess, it would probably sing and dance as your sidekick and bewitch villains into submission with (what else) brown butter cornbread.

And please don't actually retire the dough balls. That would be a tragedy. Is your grandmother the one who got you into cooking? Was it the chicken and yummy dough-based spheres that started it all? (See? That doesn't sound sexy at all.) Or was it something else? What was the first thing you made that felt like yours?

Still interested in visiting? You should be getting the official approval in the mail soon, assuming you passed your background check. (I'm sure Greg has thought of everything. He's no fool.) Once it's in your hands, you'll be able to confirm your status online and schedule a visit.

Just... No pressure. Even if you get cleared, even if everything goes through, it'll be okay if you don't come. Truly. If all we ever have are the letters, that's still more than I ever expected.

Also, congratulations on not graduating. I mean that.

You not wanting to be part of some ceremony might be your way of making your own. Your own timeline. Your own traditions. Maybe they're not exactly Nashville. Not exactly LA. Not exactly Korea. Maybe they're lard-fried mandoo in a cast iron pan, eaten off the hood of a low-rider at Griffith Park. Seems like a good kind of ceremony to me.

Your relationship with your parents sounds... unique. I can't imagine having a five-and-a-half-day disagreement with my mom. It was just me and her and she was a bit of a firebrand. Flared up easily. Forgave easily. Warm through and through. Even when she was mad at me (especially when I told her I wasn't leaving for college), there was still love in it.

I learned how to say sorry from her. Because every time I did, she'd pull me into one of those full-body, every-inch-of-arm, bury-your-face-in-her-shoulder kind of hugs. So for me, saying sorry always comes with a bear hug attached.

You said it's the unexpectedness that keeps you coming back. If we meet, does that end? If these letters and their stories step into a real room—with ID checks, vending ma-

chines, and plastic chairs–will it feel like everything's been revealed? Maybe in the flatness of paper, the mystery has depth. But once I'm in front of you–not in ink, but in person–will the mystery flatten?

In two or three letters' time, we might be sitting across from each other. That's a strange thing to think about. Stranger still that I'm looking forward to it.

And I'm grateful, preemptively, that you put hot sauce on your tacos. Otherwise I'd have to explain to my counselor how I invited a psychopath into a federal facility, and I can't afford to get more time added to my sentence.

–James

PS. Did you ever find anything out from the adoption agency? You don't have to tell me if you don't want to.

The *bulgogi* came out perfectly.

Minjee had marinated the meat the night before. At the beginning of the summer, she ardently studied each step in the massive tome she borrowed from the library. Soy sauce, sugar, garlic, sesame oil, a pear she grated to the teaspoon, exactly as instructed. But now, her third time making it, she went more by instinct. She wasn't overthinking any more, which was probably why it worked.

A few of the other counselors drifted over after their shifts. Rosalie, of course, and Elena and her roommates from next door.

Elena had been pulled into their orbit by proximity and books. Sharp cheekbones, a beauty mark on her jaw, and a big, floofy ponytail of dark curls that seemed to have its own gravitational field. She always had paperbacks spilling out of her backpack–thick, fast reads you'd find at airports or grocery store checkout lines–and Minjee had already borrowed three.

Halfway through dinner, Elena elbowed her and said, "By the way, someone asked if you were single."

Minjee blinked and looked up from her bowl. "What?"

"You know Q, like 007? That kind of nerdy guy on the physics demo team? Cute in a lanky way. Lugs around an LSAT prep book like it's his emotional support animal?"

Minjee squinted. "We talked at the parent welcome picnic, maybe?"

"Exactly. Anyway, he and I pulled pool duty yesterday, and we had time to chat. He asked a lot of questions about you. Like, are you single?" Elena grinned. "You're mysterious. People are curious."

Minjee's face froze for a millisecond.

Was she single? Well... she wasn't exactly taken. But she didn't feel like she was available.

Rosalie, half-listening to a different conversation, glanced over with a look. The kind that asked: *What are you going to say?*

"Oh. I... well, there's someone." Then she exhaled. That was true, right? Vague enough to be true.

Elena let out a mischievous chuckle. "Oh, that makes it all the better. Unrequited summer love. It's the stuff musicals are based on, right?"

She took another bite of *bulgogi* and steaming white rice, then sighed. "This is so good. Poor Q. He's missing out."

Minjee laughed it off. But later, while rinsing rice bowls in the kitchen, she thought of James' words.

"It felt like you were here a little longer. Like we got to hang out without being interrupted."

She didn't know what he looked like. Not at all. But she knew what it felt like for little James to be pulled into a full-body bear hug after saying sorry. She knew his excellence was the engine that propelled him, and the flaw that undid him. And she knew he could picture her riding shotgun in a low-rider, the LA sunset flaring behind her.

And somehow she wanted that–*him*–more than the guys who stood in front of her.

35.

Dear James,

Yes, my grandmother (mother's mother) was the one who got me into cooking. My mother hinted that she wasn't thrilled about adoption but the moment we got home from the airport, apparently I won her over. As soon as I could stand, I was poking and stirring and tasting. Always in her way. So she put me to work.

She used to say, "The biggest problem with child labor... is quality." So it was a big deal when I made red velvet cake for her, mostly by myself, and she served it to her friends at tea. When they asked where she bought it, she said, "Oh. Just a little baker I know." From her, that was basically a standing ovation.

I'm in Santa Barbara now, and I'm making friends with a little help from my trusty cast iron sidekick. We have these dinners on Friday nights. A bunch of counselors crammed into our tiny apartment. I try to make a big pot of something Korean by way of Nashville: bulgogi (the cast iron is great for this!), curry, dakdoritang. We make rice. People bring salads, beer, hummus, leftover tortilla chips, whatever they have lying around. It's kind of a potluck. But pure chaos.

I had to look up the word liminal, but I think that's the theme of the summer. I kind of love this in-between space. I don't have to have everything figured out yet, and the murky vagueness feels like a perk instead of a flaw. I don't think I want to do large, drawn-out research studies on tiny questions. I don't want to go to med school. I'm not even sure I'm ready to have a regular job and dental insurance.

I haven't gotten the approval yet, but I did my home-work on federal visitation protocol. Apparently, you're al-lowed to hug and kiss at the beginning and end of the visit. There's a part of me that thinks we should take the op-portunity. There's so little physical contact allowed, it feels strange to leave any of it on the table. But also, it would be weird, really weird, if the first time I see you is also the mo-ment we kiss. And I know it's even stranger to discuss this in advance. Like it should be spontaneous. Like we should let the moment decide.

But then again, our whole rhythm is built on days, not seconds. So, here is a thought. Consider it a proposal. If we have even half, or maybe just a quarter, of the chemistry in person that we have on paper...

I think we should kiss at the end.

Yours,

Minjee

He read the line once. Then again. Then a third time, slower.

"I think we should kiss at the end."

Not a metaphor. Not a literary device. Not some clever, layered Minjee turn of phrase.

A kiss. Like, actual lips. Physical contact. Human warmth, in public, under fluorescent lights and the sidelong glances of slightly bored COs.

He stared at the words, trying to figure out if there was some other meaning that he was too dense to catch.

"If we have even half, or maybe just a quarter, of the chemistry in person that we have on paper..."

He exhaled. That wasn't just a saying. That meant she felt it too. This wasn't just him.

He folded the letter with care, placed it back in the envelope, then pulled out the photo that lived in the pages where Gatsby reunites with Daisy.

Would she show up? Was this the girl who would walk in? The one who made red velvet cake for grannies at tea? Who sliced hippocampi for science and seasoned cast iron with soy-sugar marinades? Was this the girl who wanted to kiss him at the end of a prison visit?

His thumb grazed the edge of the photo.

He wanted her to come. He wanted to see if she was real. He wanted it too much.

But he still couldn't picture the moment. The person.

Minjee.

Not really.

36.

Dear Minjee,

Word around here is that I have a visitor this weekend. I won't assume anything. If Greg sends a girl who looks like the photo, I'll recognize you. But I suppose there is no way for you to recognize me.

Your grandmother sounds like someone I'd have liked to meet. Do you tell her about your Korean recipe experiments? What would she say about your new rituals? The chaotic potlucks and big pots of Korean-by-way-of-Nashville? Would she also be insulted by my agnosticism about the existence of "pretzel salad"?

I know I said it first, but your letter made me mull over the word "liminal." I never really know what a life is about until it ends. And right now, this feels like one of those things you don't name until it's over. Maybe your visit is the end of the liminal part. Not in a bad way. Just... the end of the floating, undefined stretch.

There's something strange about all this. In a world where people don't even bother to send an instantaneous text to break up, we're out here discussing whether we'll kiss over letters that take days to arrive. The federal government has somehow managed to be both the reason we're able to connect and the reason we're kept apart.

Still, by whatever authority is vested in me, your proposal is approved.

See you Saturday.

—James

She exhaled like she'd been holding her breath through the entire letter.

He said yes. In that clipped, wry, slightly formal way. Like approving a funding request or co-signing a loan application.

"See you Saturday."

That wasn't a feeling. That was a plan. Not a fantasy anymore. It was on the calendar.

She opened her closet. It felt dumb, maybe. To be planning an outfit. To be standing in front of her closet like this was a date. A first date.

But wasn't it? Kind of?

With a friend. A friend she'd known for nine months. A friend whose face she couldn't picture. Couldn't recognize. A friend who might be taller. Might be shorter. A friend who, up until now, had mostly existed in blue ballpoint ink on lined paper.

But also, a friend who'd given her five lives worth of himself. A friend who had somehow become one of her most intimate constants.

She pulled out a few dresses, one by one. Held them up. She reached for a sundress she wore when she just wanted to be a pretty, soft, comfy, sweet, safe version of herself. Pockets. Soft cotton. Fitted at the waist. One she might wear to go see... someone.

She picked over her pearls. The ones she got when she was 16. Tiny, imperfect, slightly off-white.

Well. It's who she was.

It was Nashville. It was Frodo. It was LA. It was cornbread and *songpyeon*. It was her.

And she was going to show up. As the whole thing.

Lompoc FCI - July 21, 2012

James

He followed the others into the visitation room, the familiar hollow slap of state-issued rubber soles against streaked linoleum echoing under the fluorescents. Mendez pointed toward a table near the wall. Metal, scratched, two bolted-down chairs across from each other. Standard.

But James didn't move right away. Because past the glass, in the reception area, on a bench just beside the check-in desk, there she was.

She hadn't seen him yet. She was looking down at something in her lap. Maybe her ID. Maybe a book. Maybe her hands. She was instantly recognizable. But the photo hadn't prepared him.

Her hair–inky, swingy, parted on one side–was flipped out just like in the picture, almost too perfectly, like a detail from a dream that had come true. And she was wearing a dress. Green and white, sleeveless, cinched at the waist, falling just below the knee. Not showy, not dramatic. But... intentional.

She looked like summer.

Not the beach kind. Not the sweat kind. The expensive kind. The kind with linen and mint and women who know how to wear heels in grass. He'd never been to the Kentucky Derby, but if he had, this is what he'd remember. She looked like she should be drinking something cold with a leafy garnish, laughing gently, placing bets.

She looked out of place here. It was like she'd brought her own sunlight into the room. Like she had the bloom of a summer garden in her bones.

She was still studying something in her lap so all he could see were her dark lashes. Her cheeks were rosy and flushed, nervous maybe. Her lips. The ones from the photo. They were here. Remarkably, all of her was here. She was real. She had come. And James was still staring.

He dragged his eyes away, barely, and walked toward the table Mendez had pointed to. Each step felt unsteady, like the floor might give out under the weight of what he wanted to feel and wasn't letting himself yet.

He sat. Palms flat on the table. Watched the door.

Was he ready for this? No.

Then, she stood up.

MINJEE

All the visitors were standing up, getting out their IDs. Minjee smoothed her hair with one hand, the pie in the other. The sundress she'd chosen had pockets, and she was quietly grateful her ID was tucked right there. Easy access, no fumbling.

"ID? You can't bring that in." A ruddy-faced guard–gently round, Coke-bottle glasses, avuncular in a way that didn't soften his authority–stopped her.

"What do you mean?" she said, handing him her ID.

"No food. No homemade food. You can only buy from the vending machines inside." He didn't look at her. Just stared at the screen, studying her ID.

Minjee didn't mean to, but her eyes pricked with tears. She caught herself. Breathed in. Softly exhaled. "It's chess pie," she said quietly.

The guard looked up, brow creased. His expression softened, just barely. A flicker of sympathy. "Sorry," he said. "It's policy. You can leave it here. Pick it up on your way out. You're clear to go in."

She set the heavy clear pie plate down on the table beside him, wrapped it in the white-and-burgundy checkered tea towel. "Do you want a slice?" she asked tentatively.

The guard had already moved on but looked back at her. "Smells great. But I can't."

But Minjee wasn't looking at the guard anymore. Or the pie. She was looking past them, because there was a face staring at her.

Tanned. Clean-shaven. Intense eyes. High cheekbones. Not boyish. A man. Someone she might've assumed was military. Someone composed. But there was something tentative in his gaze, too. Like he wasn't sure he was allowed to look.

Her breath hitched.

"You can go in," the guard prompted, the edge returning to his voice.

She walked forward on autopilot. The heels she'd worn, thick and strappy, were solid beneath her, but she couldn't feel them. Her legs weren't quite hers.

The face was closer now. He'd stood up from the metal table. His broad frame looked like he was holding his breath.

She stopped just in front of him. Not close enough to hug. Too close to shake hands.

She said it softly, a little stunned. "You're James."

He studied her eyes tenderly. He paused. A long pause. Then stepped closer, finally letting out a breath. "And you're..."

She reached out and awkwardly held his elbows, and his arms rose to meet hers. She whispered, fast, like if she didn't say it now, she never would. "I changed my mind."

They were so close now. And she was pulling him closer.

"What?" He said softly.

"You can kiss me. On the mouth."

She said it before she could think about it. Because she was seeing him. Not just a generic face, but his face. Real eyes. Deep set, but warm. A nose that was slightly long, perfectly wide. Serious brows and stern cheekbones. A strong jaw softened only by the way he was looking at her, like he couldn't believe she was real.

The kind of face that made her recall every word. The kind of face that made his squarish, careful handwriting suddenly make perfect sense. The kind of face forever associated with blue ballpoint ink and bureaucratic paper. A handsome, striking, quietly beautiful face.

And she wanted to kiss that face.

"Okay," he said. Her eyes met his chin, even in heels. So he leaned down and brought his face to hers. But stopped just a breath away.

She closed her eyes. Felt him inhale. And pause.

He kissed her gently. Off-center. A cautious press to her lower lip. She angled slightly, and for a moment, their mouths held each other.

No one knows how much time passed.

Then a throat gently cleared.

JAMES

James stepped back. Mendez was watching.

But James wasn't watching Mendez. He was looking at her. Her eyes were lighter than they were in the photo. Brighter. Deeper.

He took another breath. Just to ground himself for a second. "You're... Greg."

Her lips broke into a smile. Unguarded, unmistakable. Like it had been waiting inside the photo this whole time.

Mendez cleared his throat with a little more conviction this time.

She stepped back from him. They finally dropped their arms.

Now he could see her whole face. Her eyes crinkled. Full, pink lips. Broken into a big smile.

"You still don't believe I'm not a catfish," she said.

Those lips were saying something. He had just kissed those lips. Something he hadn't dared to imagine. But had woken up thinking about. More than once.

"Greg might've hired you," he said. "Paid you to show up. Given you a backstory."

He was talking. But he was mostly remembering her mouth. And the way she smelled. Grapefruit. And kumquats. Did he know what kumquats smelled like? Not really. But he was pretty sure they should smell like her.

Somehow, they sat.

"So you think I studied the letters? That Greg prepped me?" she whispered.

James looked up from her mouth. Her eyes twinkled like she was already writing this moment down in her head. And for the first time since she'd walked in, his brain stopped spinning. Just for a second.

He whispered back. "Greg's a genius."

Minjee pressed her palms into the table. Not shaking, just still. Shoulders a little tight, her eyes lowered. Then solemnly, "Greg will want your wallet key."

James broke into an unavoidable laugh. It rushed out of him. Fast, unfiltered. He couldn't help it.

She smiled. Smug, but also wide. Glowing.

She was real. She was like the letters. But a whole body. An expressive face. A full person.

"You've learned crypto well," he said wisely. "I see now, I've been scammed by the very best."

Her face shifted, softened. Like she'd just remembered to be apologetic. "They wouldn't let me bring in the pie," she said, a little sheepish. "I made chess pie."

James placed a hand over his heart, mock-wounded. "So Greg did plan to kill me after all."

She shook her head, eyes narrowing just slightly. "No. If that was the plan, I would've brought brown butter cornbread."

James just stared at her. Dumbfounded. Grinning like an idiot. He couldn't believe it. It was happening. In real time.

The letters had carried him through whole weeks. He'd reread them. Obsessively. From first to last. From last to first. Out of order, sometimes. He'd memorized whole sentences. Whole jokes.

And now she was just... generating this stuff on the spot. It just kept coming.

She was funny. And fast. And real. And she was here.

MINJEE

Minjee couldn't believe it. They were flirting. In a prison visitation room. Under fluorescent lights. With a guard ten feet away. And, somehow, it felt electric.

It was more than she'd let herself imagine. Seeing him. All of him.

She was suddenly grateful for the dress she'd almost talked herself out of wearing. And the pearls, her cotillion pearls. Slightly too formal, but now she was glad. They made her feel anchored. Like she'd arrived as the version of herself she hoped he'd been picturing.

Her eyes kept moving over his face. Darting, almost greedy. Not out of nerves, but because she was trying to memorize him. The slope of his cheekbone. The edge of his smile. The faint scar near his eyebrow she hadn't known about. She didn't want to miss a single thing.

It felt strange and familiar all at once. Like they had known each other for nine months. They had. But today, they'd stepped out of their letters. Stepped into something real.

She stared at his arm longer than she meant to. Lean but muscular, his forearm revealed by pushed-up sleeves. She wanted to press her fingers there, just to see if he was real.

"I can't touch you, right?" she whispered. Her voice didn't want to come out any louder than that.

The sound of his swallow seemed louder than it should have been. Just the body's own answer.

"No," he said. His voice was gentle. Tender.

She looked up at him, a flicker of doubt crossing her face. Had she said too much? Let too much slip?

But James didn't look away.

He held her gaze, steady. Like he was memorizing her too. Like he wanted to answer in a thousand different ways. His mouth parted, barely. Then, low and sure, "I've been thinking about touching you for months."

Minjee felt her throat catch. He hadn't said it like a line. He'd said it like a confession.

Now it was her turn to swallow. Her hands felt glued to the table now. Warm. Slightly damp. She didn't look away.

"You know," she said softly, "when I write to you, I usually think about what I want to say for a day or two. Then I sit and put it all down. At the beginning, I used to write it all at once. But lately... I come back to them in pieces. They take longer."

She paused. The words were tumbling now. Not shaped. Not edited.

"But this," she motioned between them, "this is so weird. I'm just saying things. Out loud. Without walking around for hours thinking about how they'll sound in your head. Do I still make sense?"

James smiled, just barely.

"You make more sense than I do," he said. "At least your words show up dressed."

Minjee tilted her head.

He gave a small shrug. "Mine are just coming out naked right now. Like, no filter. No edits. I don't even recognize them when they land. I didn't know I was going to call you Greg."

Minjee broke into a wide smile. "I will never stop loving that joke."

He looked at her with that half-smirk, a little too satisfied. "Who said it's a joke? Please send Greg my regards. His casting is... perfect."

She shook her head, feigning disapproval, but she could feel the grin tugging at her lips. She was so easily flustered by him. And when he looked at her–sometimes directly, sometimes from under his lashes–it wasn't just eye contact. It was intent. A kind of wolfish curiosity. Like he was studying her and picturing something. She felt it in her pulse.

She needed to say something. "Can you tell me what you thought when you got my first letter?"

James's eyes softened. "I simply thought you'd never write back."

Minjee laughed under her breath. "Yeah, no, I didn't think this would work either. Who writes letters in 2012? The American postal service is a marvel."

There was something about the way he moved–quiet, deliberate, a little caged–like someone used to being watched. His voice dropped slightly, even though they were already speaking in hushes. "But even in your first letter... you came through."

Minjee raised an eyebrow.

He nodded, like he was stating a fact. "You compared your institution to mine. UCLA and Lompoc. That's clearly unhinged."

She let out a short, delighted laugh. Then shook her head softly. "I remember writing that. I wasn't trying to be clever. I was just... writing. I didn't know what would come out. And I didn't think it would matter."

James tilted his head. "And I remember when you started signing your letters, *Minjee.*"

At that, something clicked into place in her. She hadn't realized he'd been paying that kind of attention

He glanced away. His shoulders–broad, but not showy–rose just slightly as he did. His khaki button up stretched across his chest. He wasn't bulky, but he was built. Like someone who had to stay sharp in tight spaces.

Then he looked back at her. Something in his expression had shifted. "And when you started signing off *Yours, Minjee.*"

She hadn't expected this part to feel so emotional. The things he remembered. The care he'd taken with her words.

She held his gaze. Steady now. "I had to," she said softly. "You told me not to write back," she said, her voice low. "So I had to write it."

A beat passed.

"*Yours,*" she said.

JAMES

James blinked.

It landed differently, hearing it aloud. The same words he'd read, over and over: "*Yours, Minjee.*" There was a time when he'd told himself not to read into it. But he'd read into it anyway. Every time.

And now, spoken in her voice, it wasn't just a word. It was something else entirely. A kind of defiance. A kind of claim.

He felt something in his chest. But he didn't let it sit. He didn't know how to. So he pivoted.

"I never answered your question," he said, quietly. "About the immigration judge."

Minjee looked at him steadily, though a quiet tightness shadowed her gaze.

He shrugged, like it didn't matter. "There's no answer. About when I'll get the ruling," he clarified. "Sometimes it takes a year. Sometimes they wait until your release date. Sometimes it's earlier. Just to ruin your day. No one really knows."

She nodded. Her fingers tapped the table once. Like she wanted to say something, but couldn't find the sentence.

"I never really heard anything useful from the adoption agency," she said finally.

And there it was.

"The one you mentioned coming out to LA for?"

"Yeah. They didn't have much. Just a name. The guy who found me. Said he found me in a small church. Near *Ulsan*."

She gave a soft, uneven breath. "It's kind of like the Detroit of Korea. Around the time I was born there was a lot of violence, police crackdowns on striking workers. I sometimes wonder if my story got touched by any of that. But who knows."

"Did they give you the name of the church?"

"Yeah. *Yuhleen moon.* Open Door." She glanced at him. "Kind of poetic, right? Maybe my biological mom, or family, or someone, thought that was a kindness. To leave me in a place named for welcome."

He didn't say anything. Just held her gaze, trying not to let too much show.

"But no address," she added. "I tried looking it up, but maybe it doesn't exist anymore. Or maybe it's just a tiny countryside church with no internet footprint."

"Still," he said. "It's a real place. You and I of all people know that things can be real even if..."

"Even if no one else can find them," she finished.

He nodded. "Even if they only exist in memory. Or paper. You were there. That church existed, for that moment."

She cleared her throat. "And now we're here."

And for a moment, it felt like they were back in the letters. Trading confessions. Half-answers. The kind of things you don't lead with, but eventually write down.

A low buzz sounded from the check-in desk. New visitors were being cleared through. The guards shifted slightly. James didn't need to look at the clock. He could feel it. Time was folding in on itself.

But he tried to ignore it.

"Did you really bring me a chess pie?" he asked, voice light. "Like... a whole pie?"

She looked briefly surprised. "Why, of course. I left it with that guard. I'll hold it up just to prove it when I get back out there." She pointed, one delicate hand gesturing toward the waiting area, the other briefly touching the string of pearls at her neck. There it was, that faint Southern lilt she slipped into sometimes.

"You actually are a debutante, aren't you?" He studied her closely.

She chuckled and reluctantly admitted, "I was *presented.*"

His eyebrows lifted. "They really do that? Like... present you to who? For what? Marriage? Dating? An auction?"

She grinned. "Historically? Yes. I think it was to signal that a girl could be courted. Publicly."

A pulse began in his jaw he couldn't quite get to stop. His shoulders were still, but he felt his heart start to tap against his ribs. She was sitting in front of him in that green and white sundress, like she was being courted. Like she was on a date.

In a prison visitation room. The table, chairs, and COs–all concrete reminders of where they were.

Still, this felt like something.

A first date?

He didn't know the rules for this. The usual markers didn't apply. They weren't sipping wine or splitting appetizers. They knew too much about each other. And what kind of first date starts with a kiss?

"So..." he began, voice a little too rough. He cleared his throat. "Is this our first date?"

Minjee looked at him, a little startled but not dismissive. She considered it.

"I'm wearing pearls, we had our first kiss." Then a pause. "We're not eating my chess pie..." She tilted her head thoughtfully. "I think the only thing that doesn't make it a *first* date is that we've been writing to each other for nine months."

James smirked. "And you teased me mercilessly in those letters."

Minjee's eyes widened. She blinked. Then laughed. "What? Mercilessly?"

"Come on," he said, leaning in just slightly. "You were awful."

And beautiful. And smart. And entirely out of my league. But he didn't say that.

James raised an eyebrow instead. "You literally wrote, and I quote, '*May you never, ever touch my brown butter cornbread.*'"

"It's sacred," she said, painfully earnest. "As I explained. It's the seasoning. In the cast iron." Then she smiled, a little self-conscious.

She was so good at being... her. He shook his head, pretending to sigh. "Unbelievable. I'm still recovering from the '*I want it. Bad.*' letter."

That letter had undone him. He hadn't been able to sleep for two nights after it arrived.

"That was ostensibly about Life Four," Minjee said, blinking at him with exaggerated innocence.

James exhaled, leaning back slightly, one hand dragging across his jaw. "You are *dangerous*."

So dangerous he couldn't tell if this whole thing was saving him or setting him up to get spiked.

"And yet you kept writing back," she said, light as air.

He looked at her then, not smiling, not teasing. Just looking.

"Of course I did," he said quietly. "You're... Frodo."

The joke landed, but something underneath it didn't feel like a joke. She was the one who carried the story. All his stories. All his lives. Who saw him clearly and kept walking toward him anyway. Who didn't flinch.

A pause. Something more serious tried to push its way in. He didn't know if she felt it too, the weight of everything they hadn't said. Whatever this was, he didn't want it to end.

"You know," he said, his voice warm, almost gentle, "for a date with no food, no touching, and no possibility of escape, this is kind of..."

"Perfect?" Minjee offered.

He nodded his head slowly. "I was going to say *unexpectedly charming*, but yeah. Let's go with perfect."

His hand moved, just slightly, like he'd forgotten where they were. Like he was about to reach across the table and touch her wrist, the way he would've if this were a first date in the real world. At a real restaurant. Without ID checks.

But he caught himself.

Instead, he folded his forearms gently across the table in front of him. A small act of containment. If he didn't, his whole heart might lurch forward and try to get to her first.

"Objectively a great date," she agreed, mock-serious. "Strong start. Memorable kiss. Above-average banter. Emotional risk-taking. What more do you want?"

James looked at her, heart thudding like a warning.

You.

But instead he said, "More time."

He didn't mean to, but his eyes flicked up, just briefly, to the wall clock behind her.

11:53. Seven minutes. Maybe less.

She noticed. Of course she did. Her smile faltered, then steadied again. Minjee glanced down at her hands, then back up at him.

"Will we still write?" Her voice was quiet. Not anxious. Just... checking.

James blinked. *Write?*

He lived for her letters. They were how he measured time now. Not by sunrises or meals or work schedules. But by her voice arriving on a page. Even when they came five days apart or two or seven. It didn't matter. Only they mattered.

Of course they would write.

But the thought of going back to that–slow words on a page, pauses between thoughts, days of silence–after this? After hearing her voice in real time, after seeing her face react without delay, after touching her, even just for seconds... It felt like giving up unlimited breath for air that only came in teaspoons.

He nodded. "Yeah. Of course we'll write." But his chest ached at the thought.

Paper couldn't hold the way her eyes crinkled when she was trying not to laugh. Or how her voice curled around a joke. Or the sharp, focused way she looked when she was serious.

Letters were everything. But now, they would be everything but *this*.

"I'm working at the science camp weekday mornings, and I'll be in the lab most afternoons," she said. "But I can come again. On a Saturday. Two weeks from now." She hesitated, then added, "I could probably come once more after that."

As if realizing the weight of her assumption, she glanced at him and asked, "Can I see you again?"

James swallowed. "Two more Saturdays?"

It was more than he could've asked for. But it was nowhere near enough.

Recovering, he nodded, voice low and steady. "So you want me to agree to two more dates?"

Minjee smiled sweetly–the kind of smile that should carry a warning label–before saying, "Yes. But I'll have to make sure Greg is willing to hire me two more times."

When James smiled–broadly, a little stupidly–she added, "And you're not allowed to make fun of my strawberry Jell-O pretzel salad."

"It's an abomination," he insisted. But held up his hands in surrender, "But I confess, I think about it more than I should."

That made her laugh, briefly. But then something in her face quieted down. She lowered her eyes and drew in a breath.

She said plainly, "I didn't think about how hard it would be to say goodbye."

James stopped. He'd just had that thought himself. Hearing her say it lit something in him. Like two neurons sparking across a synapse, a current firing clean and sharp between them. Like they'd both experienced the same flash at the same time. *How does she know?*

And then she looked up at him. Clear-eyed, unflinching.

He held her gaze. Then took the moment. "Can I kiss you goodbye?"

She didn't answer. She just stood. And he stood with her.

She stepped in, close enough that he could smell her again. That citrusy brightness, breezy and sweet. *Kumquat*, he decided. He didn't even know what kumquats really smelled like, but if they didn't smell like her, it was their loss.

"I wanted that first one way more than I was supposed to," she said. Quiet, but completely frank.

He reached for her, not rushing, just slow enough that she would see him coming. She didn't flinch. Didn't hesitate. The air between them seemed to hold its breath.

It was supposed to be chaste. Like their first. Just a parting gesture. A memory to carry back into their separate worlds.

But the second his lips touched hers, something shifted.

She made a soft noise. Surprised. Involuntary. Too real.

Then her hand was on his collar, tugging him closer. Her head tilted slightly, deepening the kiss, with a quiet kind of claim. Like something crossing over. Like all the weeks and months of letters, of ink and imagined voice and paper-thin hope, had built up to this: her mouth simultaneously saying all the words she had written and even the ones she had not.

He'd spent so long holding back. Not just his feelings but his form. He'd only existed to her in letters. Blue ink. Squarish handwriting. Careful phrasing. A version of himself he could plan, revise, control. He hadn't even let himself believe she was real.

How could she be? He was in prison. She was not. She had H Mart and rat brains and *songpyeon*, lecture halls, roommates, a best friend waiting outside. He had four concrete walls and too much time.

So he held back. Even tried to push her away. Told her not to write back.

And then she did.

Yours, Minjee.

And now she was here. In his arms. Pulling him in.

Not saying *yours*. Saying *mine*.

She was the one deepening the kiss. Her mouth was warm and certain. Inviting. Possessing.

He exhaled into her, dizzy with the feel of her, *the colossal vitality of her.*

"Shin." Mendez's voice. Terse. Unapologetic.

She froze. They both did.

Then she pulled back. Breathed in, held it.

Exhaled.

Part 4

Seoul

Present Day

Dohyun finished his worksheets in record time. The last answer was a little messy, but if he snuck out while his mom was still in the kitchen, he might just get away with it.

He grabbed Frodo's leash. "(Come on), Frodo," he whispered. "(Only twenty minutes. We'll be back before dinner.)"

Frodo thumped his tail once. He'd follow Dohyun into any adventure. The playgrounds, community parks, stairwells below the skyrise apartments were their frontier.

Dohyun jammed on his sneakers–stepping on the habitually-bent back heels, half-tying the laces–and slipped into the hallway. The apartment was high, and the elevator took forever. But today, it came right away.

Dad was inside! Coming home. "(Going down now? How about dinner?)" he asked.

Dohyun grinned. "(20 minutes!) I promise. *Daktoritang* for dinner. I'm not missing that."

Frodo wriggled like he was going to explode. Dohyun bent to fix his heels. And right then, the dog bolted, cheerfully following Dad back down the hall.

"Frodo!" Dohyun yipped and chased after him.

The apartment door was half-open. He pushed it wide. And there they were.

Mom's hand was curled in Dad's shirt collar. Pulling his face down. They were kissing. Like, really kissing. Not a peck.

"Ugh," Dohyun said, loud enough.

They laughed. Didn't even stop.

He grabbed Frodo by the collar and pulled him back out.

"(20 minutes!)" he shouted from the hallway.

Santa Barbara/ Lompoc - 2012

37.

Dear James,

I wanted to write back right away. I really did. But there was so much. And somehow, all of it felt too big and too weird and too close to put into words. Like trying to describe the ocean while you're still treading water.

Now I'm wondering if I should've at least sent a quick thank you note. I mean, technically, you hosted me. And etiquette says a guest should always write one.

So... thank you. For the date. It was strange and wonderful, and I haven't stopped thinking about it.

What's strange now is that when I sit down to write, I can imagine your face so vividly. Before, you were a vague person-shaped shadow in my mind. Now I see you. I imagine you listening.

I didn't have a photo, but I knew it was you from across the room. Your face matched your letters. I mean, probably because you recognized me first. But I can't help but think that if someone lined up ten guys and said, "Pick James from the letters," I would've picked you. Or at the very least, I would've wanted it to be you.

I'm sorry if I was weird... on our date. Half of my brain was just yelling "act normal!" the whole time. I know I kept staring at your arm. It was right there across the table. Something I could almost reach. I just kept looking at this one vein, running across your forearm, and all I wanted to do was trace it. To see if it was real. To see if you were.

Oh, and you asked about this in a letter, and I completely forgot to explain it. So here goes:

The striatum is this weird, tucked-away structure deep in the brain. It's not in the wrinkly part that people usually think of when they picture "the brain." It's buried. Unsung. But it's connected to movement, control, and reward. It's like a hidden switchboard that helps coordinate what you want with what you do.

If I had to guess? Something like our last kiss probably lit mine up.

I think this letter's going to arrive too close to our next visit for you to write back in time. But remind me to tell you about the time I tried to make tteokbokki. Spoiler: it did not go well.

Also, you said your sentence was 18 months. How much of that have you served? Just curious.

Yours,

Minjee

P.S. I have a confession. I'll tell you in person. Nothing illegal. But possibly humiliating. For me.

James held the letter like it might set something off. Not an alarm, exactly. Something quieter. Like a tripwire.

It was always like this with her now. She didn't write like someone trying to get to know him. Or impress him. Or entertain him. She wrote like someone letting him in backstage. And somehow, that was worse.

He read it slowly. Not because it was long. Only because he didn't want to miss anything. And when he got to the part about her and his vein, it knocked the air out of him.

She could've written about wanting to make out. Or what she wasn't wearing. Or whatever else some guy in prison might want.

But no. She wrote about his arm. A vein. The distance between a fingertip and the skin. And it was so much worse than anything explicit. Because it was real. And close.

He closed his eyes. Played it back. He could almost feel her breath, the way her fingers hovered, the soft tug of her hand on his collar. Her lips on his. And that should've been enough. It was already more than he'd let himself want.

But now that he'd had it, just that sliver of her, he wanted more. He wanted her fingertips on his arms. He wanted his hand on her wrist. In her hair. On her cheeks.

He didn't remember her staring at him. Probably because he was too busy staring at her. How her cheeks lifted when she smiled. How her whole face joined in–her eyes, the hint of dimples, the stillness she held when she looked at him. Like she could actually see right through him.

He remembered having to look away. Not dramatically. Just enough to breathe. Just enough to reset.

Near the bottom, her handwriting tilted slightly, trying to cram it in: *"Also, you said your sentence was 18 months. How much of that have you served?"*

He stared at it for a long time.

She was wondering. Maybe she was doing the math. Maybe she was picturing what happens after.

She shouldn't. He couldn't. Not with the immigration ruling still hanging over his head. Not with the possibility that he might not just leave prison, but leave the country. Leave her.

He could feel the ground shifting. Because he was still falling. And there might be a long way down. And he couldn't take her down with him.

At the end of the letter, she mentioned a confession. Nothing illegal. Possibly humiliating. For her.

Maybe it should've made him smile. But all he had were questions: A boyfriend? A secret? Regret?

It was probably nothing. But time stretched everything. A little curiosity became a thread, became a loop, became a knot. And now he was in it, twisting it over and over in his head.

A confession. Was she dating someone else? Was she an undercover DEA agent? Was she in a cult? Was she... actually hired by Greg?

And yet, he couldn't stop thinking about her hand, just a finger, tracing his arm. That was the part that stayed. The part that looped in his brain when things went quiet. The part he woke up to.

Lompoc FCI - August 4, 2012

MINJEE

Minjee and Rosalie wriggled around in the front seats of Rosalie's ancient Honda Civic, parked in a far corner of the lot, for decency, under the shade of a tree, for the heat.

Minjee managed to trade out her cutoff jean shorts for Rosalie's long khaki pants, tugging them on with some effort.

"You owe me for this," Rosalie muttered, shimmying into the tiny shorts with visible regret.

"They're breezy," Minjee offered.

"They're denim underwear."

Minjee didn't argue. She'd read the prison dress code twice. No tank tops. No shorts. No exceptions. If she didn't change, she wouldn't get in to see James. And no way was she making it all the way to Lompoc just to be turned away because of a rule about visible knees.

She was still wearing her bright yellow Camp Sci Revolution! polo, cheerfully embroidered with a stylized atom and the phrase: "Get up and atom!" *Oh geez.* Was that a glitter and glue stain left over from a camper's experiment?

She'd meant to wear something nicer. A long red floral wrap dress with loose puffy sleeves. Her strappy espadrilles. Dangly earrings. But the bag she'd packed with all of it had been left behind at the university center, locked in the gear closet where Camp Sci Revolution usually stored supplies. Everyone had gone straight to the beach cleanup. And by the time they realized, it was too late.

So now she was wearing white Vans (no socks), rolled up khakis (a size too long), and the most fluorescent pun-based shirt on planet Earth. Underneath it all, the blue-striped bikini she'd worn into the ocean that morning. The string tied behind her neck peeked out from under the collar.

She'd tried to towel off in the car, but everything was still a little damp. Her hair was up in a messy bun. Her bangs stuck to her forehead.

She didn't bring pie this time. Just herself. Camp counselor. Beach litter-picker-upper. Brain expert for the sixth-grade set. Girl with a confession.

Well, it was probably good he saw her like this. Right?

When she reached the waiting area, she saw him through the glass. James. Already sitting. Already scanning. Broad shoulders, clean lines, that calm strength in his posture. Like someone who knew how to hold tension without showing it. But when he saw her, he broke into a smile, wide and unguarded, and raised one hand in greeting.

She waved back, heart skipping at the sheer dorkiness of it. They looked like middle schoolers at the end of summer. Like two weeks apart had felt like years. Like they were brimming with enthusiasm. Dorky, dorky enthusiasm. She bit her lip to keep from grinning too hard. Tried to walk normal. Not run. Not skip. Just walk.

When she stepped into the room, James was standing. He looked like he'd been waiting to catch her.

She walked right up to him but didn't step into his arms. Not yet.

Instead, she reached for his arms first. Ran her hands slowly up from his wrists to his forearms. Tan, smooth, solid under her touch. Her fingertips brushed over warm skin, the familiar line of a vein she'd imagined a hundred times in her head. She let out a little sigh.

"I wanted to do this," she murmured. "Last time."

Then she leaned in, rising onto her toes, and kissed him. Slow and deliberate. Not at all shy.

One of his hands rose, cupping her cheek as he kissed her back. Grounding her. Holding her like something he'd been picturing for a long time.

She felt it. In her chest. In her knees. All the way down.

When they pulled apart, he was still close. Still smiling.

"I wanted to do this," he said. "Exactly this."

And then they sat, like it was the most natural thing in the world.

JAMES

"Are you coming straight from camp?"

Minjee looked down at her shirt and laughed. "What gave it away? Was it the screaming yellow polo? Or the atom with a smiley face on it?"

He read outloud, "Get up and... atom." And then smiled with his eyebrows raised.

She rolled her eyes. "Today was beach cleanup day. Full chaos. Half the campers left their crocs somewhere on the beach and a few were so worn that they got put into a trash bag like they were litter. One lost a retainer. We picked up more cigarette butts than you'd think is humanly possible." She wrinkled her nose. "And after the hundredth one, you stop being grossed out by the fact that a stranger once had it in their mouth." Then, cheerfully, "Don't worry. I washed my hands."

She said it all with a kind of breezy delight, her eyes crinkling when she laughed.

And James, who not long ago had only known her as imagined voice on paper, just sat there, drinking her in. Not staring. Not devouring. Just... taking in the fact that he could. Like water after too long without.

Her hair was piled up high in a bun, messy in the way that made him smile. It bared the soft line of her neck, the sharp clean cut of her jaw. He could imagine following those lines with his nose. And her bangs, clearly too long, kept sweeping into her lashes, framing her eyes, her mouth. That mouth that had just been on his a moment ago.

And then there were the little tendrils of hair that had escaped her bun and curled against her temples. Like someone had pulled her close. Like she'd just been kissed.

And, before he could stop himself, "Are you wearing a swimsuit under that?"

Minjee blinked. Then turned toward him, her expression somewhere between amused and betrayed. "...Are you asking me what I'm wearing underneath my clothes?"

James opened his mouth. Nothing came out. He inhaled. Tried again.

"I mean... I didn't mean... I just noticed the..." He pointed vaguely at the back of his own neck.

She tugged lightly at the string behind hers.

"Oh right. That."

Then, deadpan, "Are we about to enter b-r-a territory?"

James laughed—part relief, part fluster, part *oh-God-she-caught-me*. Leaning back slightly, he raised both hands in mock surrender. "Fine, I rescind the question."

Minjee smiled, still a little pink in the cheeks, but clearly enjoying that she'd won that round.

"A wise man once warned me that a college girl should... be careful about what she brings up," she said.

Then, offhand, "Since I didn't score the wallet key last time, Greg was hoping the bikini would be the clincher."

James shook his head and laughed. "That guy knows how to play me."

Minjee chuckled and went on. "It wasn't planned. I wasn't trying to—" She shrugged. "Everyone got dunked at the end of the cleanup. It was chaos. So much sand and screaming. I was soaked and didn't even have my own towel. Hey, do you want a coffee?"

Minjee stood and pointed toward the vending machines.

James nodded like he did. Which he mostly did. But mostly, he watched her walk away.

The polo shirt swayed just slightly with her steps. Her messy and perfect bun bounced once.

The bikini string trailed behind her neck, a slash of blue against yellow polyester. And on the back of her shirt–just faintly, just enough–he could see the darker imprint of damp fabric clinging to the shape of her bikini. The outline of the straps. The curve of her back.

His brain, traitorous as ever, took this as a challenge. It said, "*Oh! I see what you mean!*" And promptly stripped away what he could see, down to the bare core of what he wanted. Picturing the shirt peeled off and dropped on the sand. Replacing khakis with smooth, sun-wet skin. Imagining her in the ocean. Dripping. Laughing. Flushed from sun, salt, and motion.

He could see it. The blue-striped bikini. The pink cheeks. That smile.

He shifted slightly in his seat.

"You want a latte or anything?" Minjee called.

James exhaled, grateful for the interruption. Possibly the first time in recorded history, anyone had felt grateful for vending machine coffee. "Sure," he said. "Sounds great."

He looked over. She was crouched in front of the vending machine, studying the options like they were clues in a logic puzzle. Even under the loud polo and baggy khakis, she looked effortlessly lithe. Compact, light on her feet, and athletic in a way that made it hard not to notice. And it didn't help that he'd just imagined her soaked and laughing in a damn bikini.

"Are you more of a peanut M&Ms or a Funyuns guy?" she said over her shoulder. "Oh, and there's one last Jalapeño Cheetos!"

James blinked, then pulled on a smile. "You had me at fake onion rings."

MINJEE

Minjee returned with her haul, arms full of snacks and instant lattes that probably had more powder than coffee.

"I think I'm kind of starving from the beach clean-up," she said, dropping into her bolted seat across from him.

She started opening bags like a true camp counselor, fingers moving quickly as she handed him a latte and tore into the Funyuns. Something about it–the ease of sitting with him, the salt in her hair, the faint ache in her shoulders–made the visit feel strangely light.

"Doesn't today feel... almost easy?" she said, tossing him a bag of chips.

"I was so nervous last time. After I saw you–saw what you looked like, heard your voice–I went back and reread all your letters. And now..." She glanced at him, then back into another bag, smiling to herself. "It kind of feels like we've hung out in person more than once. Like this isn't the second time. Just... familiar."

She shrugged, the gesture small and half-apologetic. "Maybe it's because I look like a total mess today."

He looked like he was about to say something–something more–but instead he simply said, "I like this look."

One of her eyebrows arched, slow and suspicious. She genuinely looked like chaos. Hair stiff from salt and wind, skin a little too shiny, her shirt stretched and damp in all the wrong places.

What look? This one?

But he wasn't joking. He was gazing at her. Not in the cinematic, sweeping way that might've made her flinch or look away. Just in a quiet, steady way that made her believe him. Like he meant it. Like it was true and he was only saying it out loud.

He picked up a Funyun, turned it over thoughtfully in his fingers. "It's both surreal and... comfortable," he said, a little sheepishly. "I still can't believe we get to hang out in person. And I can't believe this is only our second time. It feels like we've had a million conversations already."

Minjee let out a short laugh. Half surprise, half delight. He might've been looking at her mouth when she did. And weirdly, she didn't feel self-conscious. She just felt... amused. Present. Maybe just plain happy.

She reached into the bag and pulled out a chip that would taste vaguely like freeze-dried jalapeño. "I had a whole list of things I wanted to tell you," she said. "All week, I kept thinking, *'Oh, I should tell him that on Saturday.'* I was treating today like one long letter I was going to write." She laughed again, this time more to herself. "But now? I can't remember any of it."

A smile crept across his face. The kind that tried not to be a smile but gave itself away anyway.

"Yeah? You were saving things to tell me?"

"But I seriously can't remember a single thing," she said.

She looked at him again. Too directly this time. She just liked his face. Liked looking at it. The way his eyebrows pulled slightly when he was listening. The warmth behind his eyes. And honestly? He had a ridiculously pleasing nose.

She had to glance away to finish the thought.

"All I remember is that I already told you what a striatum is."

James let out a soft, easy laugh. His shoulders bounced just slightly and Minjee tried not to stare. But something about the sound of it made her chest feel lighter. Like her body wanted to laugh too.

"Oh wait! I remember," she said, brightening. "I was going to tell you about one of my epic fails in Korean cooking."

He looked at her, half-smiling. "Your magic cast iron failed you?"

"Well... I failed me. I should've just followed the directions."

"What did you make?"

Oh God. She was going to have to just say it. She knew it was wrong.

"*Tuck-bock-ee?*" she said, squinting one eye shut like she was bracing for impact. She was smiling. Grimacing. Something in between.

James blinked. "Oh my God."

Then a grin broke across his face, quick and sly. Like it ran out the door before he could stop it. Almost immediately, he tried to reel it back in. Lips pressed together, cheeks tightening like he was stifling a sneeze.

The smile stayed, but smaller now. Muted. His eyes were warm, almost apologetic. Like he knew he shouldn't be this amused but couldn't quite help it.

"This whole time, reading your letters, I always imagined you saying these dishes in a perfect Korean accent. I should've realized..."

He grinned and leaned in slightly, voice low and teasing. "How do you say the thing you eat during *Chuseok*?"

Her eyes went wide. She covered her face with both hands. "No!" she gasped, laughing now, loud and mortified.

She peeked at him between her fingers, and yep. He was grinning. Watching her. Looking like he was having the best time.

It filled her up. Disarmed her. Made her feel a little warm under her cheeks and collarbone.

Normally, this–getting it wrong, sounding wrong, *being* wrong–would've mortified her. It certainly used to. But not with him. James had shared so much with her: his lives, his ugly truths, his pride in terrible things. He made it feel like the cracks let the light in just as much as the polished parts reflected it.

And more than anything, she wanted to know. To learn. To let someone teach her something about herself she didn't already know.

He was still chuckling when he said, "It's *ddukk-bbokki*."

"Wait—it starts with a D?" she asked, pulling her hands down slowly, her smile blooming without permission. Curious. Open. "There's a T in all the cookbooks..." She visualized it: *tteokbokki*. That weird double-T she'd always squinted at.

"I always wondered what a 'tt' is supposed to sound like..."

He tilted his head, amused. "It's like... a hard D. Not *duh*, but something between a D and a T. Like... *dtuh*."

"*Ddukk-bokki*," she repeated, lips pursed in concentration like she was trying to nail a final exam.

"The B is the same way. It's like a hard B. Press your lips together tight before saying it. Like *bbokki*." Then he watched her mouth. Smiling a little. Like he didn't mind having an excuse to look.

"*Ddukk-bbokki*," she said cautiously.

He smiled again, nodding, clearly pleased. "Pretty good. But what made it an 'epic fail'?"

She sighed, maybe just a wee bit dramatically. "I treated the rice cakes like pasta. Waited until the water boiled, then dropped in the—"

"Oh." He gave her an amused look, subtle, but like he already knew where this was headed. "So it was watery."

Her jaw dropped. "Yes! How did you know?"

He let out a soft laugh, the kind that came with a small shake of his head. "It's the one Korean dish I actually know how to make. I've done that too, just forgot to put the *dduk* in at the start. You need the starch to thicken everything. It's like... Korean food 101."

She looked at him, smiling like she'd just won something. This was... fun. Learning things from him. Laughing with him. Watching his face animate as he talked. Having him tease her. Teach her. Look at her like he was still trying to make sense of the fact that she was here. Like she was someone he hadn't expected to be real, but somehow, still was.

JAMES

He wished he could make *tteokbokki* for her. It was the one halfway-decent thing he could cook. Apparently last time, she'd made him her chess pie. He hadn't stopped thinking about it since.

Then Minjee winced suddenly, pressing her fingers to her temple like she was trying to push a thought out of her skull.

"I'm a little embarrassed, but I have a confession," she said.

James raised an eyebrow. "Right. You mentioned that. Should I be sitting down?"

"You're already sitting."

"I believe you said it wasn't illegal?"

Her eyes were mildly horrified. "No, no. Nothing like that."

He didn't think it was, not really. But his pulse still ticked up. *Greg really did hire her. She scams inmates for Bitcoin. She has a burner wallet and a dark web handle. It's fine. We can still be friends, right?*

She exhaled. Opened her palms like she was bracing for impact. Looked him dead in the eye.

"So... there's this guy at camp. Q. He's–"

"Your boyfriend?" James asked, a little too fast.

"No!" she said quickly, eyes wide. "He... expressed interest. Persistent interest."

James tilted his head. "Persistent?"

Of course he was persistent. James instantly, instinctively hated this guy.

She waved a hand. "He kept tracking me down. Like, I had compost duty all week, and suddenly he was really into compost. Volunteered for lunch duty during my shift. Then again for three consecutive shifts. Kept bringing me Kind bars. I think that's some kind of camp love language?"

James didn't answer. *Kind bars.* He was too busy trying not to grin.

"I told him there was someone," she said. "Trying to let him down easy."

"And?"

"He nodded. Like he was calculating odds. And then he goes, 'Okay, who is he? What's his name?'"

She spread her hands. "I said, 'You don't need to know that.'"

James raised an eyebrow.

"And then he goes, 'How come I've never seen him?' And finally, oh God, he said, 'I think I can take him.'" She gave him a withering look. "Like it was a duel."

James blinked, his expression caught between confusion and contempt. "*I think I can take him?*"

"I panicked!" she said, half-laughing. "So I told him my boyfriend was in jail."

James stared at her.

"And that he might not love it if word got around that some guy was bothering me."

There was a beat.

"That's the confession?" he said.

She nodded, sheepish. "I may have... strongly implied you were my incarcerated, potentially violent boyfriend."

James tried to play it cool. He really did. But something warm and ridiculous rose in his chest anyway.

He laughed to himself, then recovered. "So you're running a boyfriend scam now?"

She put her face in her hands. "I'm so sorry."

Sorry? For what? For calling him her boyfriend? For implying he was in jail for violent offenses instead of interstate commerce law? For suggesting he might be the kind of guy who got possessive about her?

He looked at her, eyes glinting. "You're out there expanding the range of fraud you engage in. I respect it."

Minjee laughed, but there was an underlying flicker of something. That little heart-shaped face of hers carrying the weight of genuine embarrassment.

Kind of as a joke, only kind of, he leaned in mock-serious and purred, "You know... you didn't have to make it up. I would've said yes."

Minjee blinked. "Yes to what?"

He shrugged, still close, still smiling. "Being your boyfriend. Maybe you should tell that guy your boyfriend got locked up for what he did to the last guy who gave you Kind bars."

He looked up, thoughtful now, mock-considering. "And I'd be happy to kick his ass if you needed such a service."

Then he crossed his arms, and his biceps flexed just slightly, just enough. Like he was thinking through the logistics of throwing Q into a compost heap. "Who knows?" he grinned cocky and shameless. "I might even enjoy it."

She looked at him for a long moment. Something quieted in her eyes.

"Then let's do it," she said.

James froze, just slightly. The smile still on his face, but caught there now. "Wait. Do what?"

She looked at him with no emotion. "Be boyfriend-girl-friend."

He furrowed his brows. "You actually want me to be your boyfriend?"

Minjee tilted her head, her voice gentler now. "I think that's why I blurted it out," she said. "It was easy to say it because... it already felt true."

He nodded slowly. He didn't answer right away. Then, finally, "If I were the kind of guy you should have as a boyfriend, someone worthy of you..." He trailed off.

She looked at him. Steady. "But you're not?"

"I want to be," he said. "More than I can say. Because you deserve someone good. No. Someone great. Accomplished."

A pause. Then quieter. "Someone who can actually show up. Take you out. Be seen with you in daylight." He blinked slowly. Always hammering the final nail in his own coffin. "Someone who is not in federal prison."

She was silent for a moment, just staring down at her hands. Then she looked up, something calm and certain settling behind her eyes. "But I still want to call you my boyfriend."

James exhaled. A soft, uneven laugh. "Then do it. Call me your boyfriend. Tell that Q guy and anyone else that you've got a boyfriend. And it can be me. Just..." His voice dropped. "If you ever need to let me go, don't hesitate. Break up with me. Send a 'Dear James' letter."

Minjee smiled–slow, sweet, a little sad. She understood him in that moment. That he would make it easy for her to leave. That he wouldn't ask her to stay, even if it broke him.

Then something flickered across her face. A shift. "Wait," she said. "Isn't that just how... normal boyfriends work?"

James laughed again, this time with his head tilted back, eyes on the ceiling.

"No, that's not–" He broke off, smiling at his own impulse. "I mean, if you meet someone. If you get bored. If life just takes you somewhere else. Whatever the reason." He fixed his dark eyes at her, so full of sincerity. "I'll always be glad. *Grateful* even. That you once considered me your boyfriend."

There was a pause. Then a twinkle sparked in her eye. "Wait. Did you already break up with me?" Minjee asked, grinning.

James closed his eyes and laughed, part exasperation, part genuine amusement at his own inability to communicate like a functional human being.

"So let me recap," Minjee said, her voice dry but her eyes warm. "We are now officially boyfriend-girlfriend. Starting immediately. But I can break up with you at any time."

She looked at him expectantly, like she was daring him to object.

"And you can break up with me," she added, "also at any time. Like a normal couple."

James sighed, almost defeated by the clarity, the sweetness, the frank logic of it all. "Yeah... that covers it. Except we have to break up via letters. Which makes us sound like we're dating during the Civil War."

Minjee lit up. "Oh! I've got it. If you want, we can back-date any breakups to the moment the letter was written."

James laughed genuinely, helplessly. "You think I'm worried about the mail interfering with the timing of our breakups?"

MINJEE

A low buzz echoed from the far wall, followed by the heavy thunk of a lock releasing.

"Well," she said, standing and gathering up the snack wrappers, "that was a productive date."

She didn't look at him. She could feel the smile on her face and didn't quite trust it.

Boyfriend.

Not exactly how people typically become boyfriend-girlfriend. But a version shaped across nine months of letters. And two visits. A strange little pocket of existence with its own rules, its own rhythm. She'd take it.

James stood, the smile still playing at the corners of his mouth. He exhaled. Almost a laugh, almost surrender. "You really are going to be the death of me."

She opened her mouth to tease him again. *You're my boyfriend now. You have to kiss me goodbye.* But before the words could form, he moved.

Just a step. But it was fast. Sure. Like he'd already decided.

Minjee barely had time to react before his hands found her waist, firm and steady, pulling her toward him. And just like that, her arms looped around his neck. Automatic. Certain. Like her body already knew the choreography.

There was no hesitation. No nerves. No question marks. Just a clean, perfect collision–like a ball thwacking into a mitt, like a chord resolving exactly where it should.

Her pulse stuttered, then settled. Not from nerves. From knowing.

His lips were warm and familiar. But his grip at her waist, possessive, was new. There was hunger in it now, edged into the corners of the kiss. But it wasn't rushed. It wasn't the kind of hunger that burned to consume. It was steadier than that. Surer. The kind that was now willing to fight for its place. Like he'd accepted the title now. *Boyfriend*.

When they pulled apart–barely, reluctantly–Minjee let her forehead rest against his without thinking. Her eyes stayed closed a moment longer than necessary.

She just stood there, holding on. Quietly stunned by how easy it had felt. Like they'd done it a hundred times. Like they could do it a hundred more.

Lompoc/Santa Barbara - 2012

38.

Dear Minjee,

I wanted to say thank you. For our time together. I know this is going to be the last visit. And even though it's far fewer than I wish we had, I'm grateful. You reminded me that the world is still good. And you've been... good. So good.

I'm also writing because I want you to ccme without having to plan what comes after. Just to help us both hold this right. I want to meet you with nothing in our hands but the moment. No plans. No next step. Just us.

So yes, you can call me your boyfriend for as long as you want. (I'm not seeing anyone else, if that wasn't clear.) But if you knew what was good for you, you'd go. You'd let this be enough. You'd call it what it was: something strange and real and maybe exactly what we both needed. And then, you'd let it end.

You'd give someone out there (maybe not that prick Q, but someone) a shot. You'd see if he's worth making your strawberry Jell-O pretzel salad for. (I picked that example very carefully. I don't think it's double-entendre-proof, but if anyone could turn it into one, it would be you.)

You called your dduk-bbokki an epic fail because it turned out watery. I've been thinking about that. Minjee, if watery rice cakes are your idea of epic, you might need to recalibrate. I ran an operation that violated, among other things, multiple interstate commerce laws. Now I spend my days in a jumpsuit issued by the federal government. That's epic.

You? You've lived a life that's been, by design, small. Controlled. Gentle on the edges. And I get why. You wanted to be the kind of daughter your parents could point to and say, "Yes, we made the right choice." You built a life around being easy to love. Easy to explain.

And somehow, I truly don't know how, you found a way to take a risk like this: You chose me. You linked your name to mine. That's not brave. It's reckless. It's ill-advised. It's borderline absurd. Maybe even, your most epic fail.

And yet, it might be the most epic thing anyone's ever done for me. I don't know how to carry that. But I'm trying.

You–your letters, your visits–made something real where I didn't think anything real could live. It's like that Open Door church. Even if no one ever finds it again, it still happened. We happened. And I'll carry that with me. Always.

–James

P.S. I know I once suggested you don't mention bras in your letters. (Still a good rule.) I should probably add that you shouldn't wear a bikini under your clothes, either. It's far too... effective.

Minjee handed Elena a jar of bulgogi marinade, the lid tight, a yellow Post-it slapped on top with neat handwriting: *"Marinate ½ pound beef (sliced thin) overnight. Add sliced onions if you want. Cook in nonstick pan, med heat. Miss you Elena!"*

Elena held it like it was precious. "This looks like a bribe."

"It is," Minjee said. "I'm trying to earn couch privileges."

She'd already returned the novels she'd borrowed though wasn't quite sure how the third one ended. Bagged up a few snacks, half a bottle of sesame oil, a set of Tupperware she knew Elena could use. She was giving things away like someone who didn't expect to come back. But in her mind, she was already trying to figure out how to.

Elena leaned against the doorway, arms crossed. "So. A boyfriend at Lompoc, huh?" She grinned. "How the hell did that happen?"

Minjee blinked, caught off guard by the phrasing. *A boyfriend at Lompoc.* How *did* that happen?

And yet, somehow, it made complete sense. That James would be her boyfriend. That she'd want to call him that. It felt... natural. As if her mind had known it before her mouth did.

She gave Elena a crooked smile. "Long story. I'll tell you one day. But I basically catfished him into it."

Elena laughed as she grabbed the trash bag from under the sink. "Wait, you? *You're* the catfish?" She shook her head as she headed for the door. "We're gonna need a couple of beers for that story."

Minjee opened the fridge and began rearranging containers to make room for the marinade and a few other ziplocked offerings. The light buzzed softly as she worked.

She knew what James was doing. What that letter was. James was preparing her for the end.

And she was supposed to drive back to LA with Rosalie on Saturday after the visit, like it was over. Like it was done.

But she couldn't help it. She found herself already planning a return.

Just as Elena stepped back inside, Minjee poked her head out of the fridge. "Hey, if I come up to Santa Barbara in a few weeks, can I crash on your couch for the weekend?"

Elena didn't even pause. She walked over, slung an arm easily around her shoulders, and proclaimed, "Definitely. I'll tell everyone the brown butter cornbread is back in town."

They both laughed.

From the living room, someone called out, "Movie's starting!" The opening notes of an overly dramatic Marvel movie filled the apartment.

Elena steered them toward the couch with a nudge. Minjee let herself be pulled along.

Inside her head, James's words circled: *"Let this be enough... Let it end..."*

James wanted her to walk away. But he should know better. Greg wasn't done yet.

Lompoc FCI - August 18, 2012

JAMES

They moved him to the camp. Apparently there was a level a touch lower than minimum security. Technically a privilege. In practice, it just meant no fences and a longer walk to a different visitation building.

The room was just as large but quieter here. Less metal, less echo. Hard plastic chairs arranged side-by-side in four-tops like a crappy fast food restaurant. One where you could only get food from vending machines.

But still, there was the possibility. You could sit close enough to pretend. Close enough to forget, for a little while.

The door buzzed.

He looked up. And whatever breath he'd been holding in reserve just... left him.

She wasn't in the bright yellow polo this time.

Her hair looked different, almost wavy. Not flipped out like usual. Styled, somehow. Like she'd just come in from a windy shoreline.

She wore a red floral dress, loose and flowing, puffed at the sleeves and wrapped at the waist. It moved when she walked, shifting just enough to reveal a glimpse of one leg, then hiding it again. Like the dress had its own rhythm, offering flashes and taking them back.

The hem caught slightly on her shoes, ballet-like things tied at the ankles with thick, off-white ribbons. Not made for walking, but somehow making every move look intentional.

She walked toward him with anticipation in every step, eyes bright, trying not to smile too big, too soon. She looked like summer trying to behave.

He stood.

And she didn't hesitate. She walked straight into his arms and tilted her face up, already rising to meet him. Her hands cupped the back of his neck. Firm, sure.

But his hands framed her waist with the kind of care you'd use to lift something precious, something he couldn't afford to drop.

He kissed her slowly. Eyes closed. Anchoring himself in it. Memorizing the shape of her mouth, the angle of her chin, the softness of her breath just before contact. Not yet desperate. But already haunted.

He felt the ache in it, deep and quiet. The kind that only comes when you know every second is borrowed.

But then her fingers slid into his hair. Threaded through. Bold. Certain. She tugged him closer with an insistence that flipped his stomach.

He inhaled sharply through his nose. This was hotter than it should've been. Not frantic. Controlled, deliberate. A provocation.

Her mouth opened against his with a confidence that rattled him. Like she wasn't saying goodbye. Like she was daring him to believe there was still more. That this wasn't their last visit.

His fingers clenched at her waist, gripping the ribbon of her dress like it anchored her to him.

Then he thought: *fuck it.*

And he let his hands move. Across her back. Down the curve of her spine. Over the soft heat of her dress, the slope of her waist.

He wanted to memorize it. Not just the shape of her, but the dare. The challenge wrapped in want. The almost-question of it: *Can you meet me here?*

The room blurred. The world blurred. Everything but her.

Like it was the beginning. Like it was the end. Because it was both.

MINJEE

They had just sat down, but neither of them moved much.

Minjee could still feel the imprint of his mouth on hers. The heat of it. The open want. His hands, roaming over her like something had finally broken open. Like some quiet restraint, long kept and well-trained, had suddenly given way. Like a boundary had been breached.

Now they were seated across from each other at a scratched-up plastic four-top, both a little flushed, both breathing just a bit too heavily for two people technically doing nothing.

She didn't look away. Neither did he. Just the two of them, staring into each other's darkened eyes, not speaking. Not wanting to. Not yet.

Because if they said something, anything, then maybe time would start moving again. The minutes would begin to fall, one by one, like cards slipping into a slot. Each one spent. Each one gone. And at the end of the entire deck, there would be a goodbye.

But if they stayed quiet, if they just held the silence, maybe time would stay still too.

James took a deep breath then started, "One. F as in Fox-trot. T as in Tango. Lowercase a as in Alpha... are you getting this down?"

Minjee blinked back. *What was he doing?*

She frowned. "What?"

"My Bitcoin wallet key," he replied solemnly.

For a second, she just stared at him.

Wait, did he need her to–

And then it hit her.

Greg.

Her eyes went wide. A sound came out of her–half cough, half laugh–like her brain short-circuited on the way to a response. More bursts followed, sputtering and breathless, like disbelief breaking loose in her throat.

James continued, unbothered.

"Where was I? I'll just start from the beginning. One, F, T, lowercase a, four, lowercase e as in-"

She wasn't even hearing him anymore. Because then came the real laughter–sharp and ragged, building fast. Her chest shook. She doubled over, clutching her stomach, gasping for air.

Oh my God. He just kept going. Like this nonsense string of letters and numbers was what she had put a wrap dress on for.

"Please stop," she wheezed, cheeks aching from the sustained attack. She wiped her eyes, still laughing, still losing it. "You're insane!"

He sat back, hands folded on the table like a smug, handsome troll. "It's the end of the game. Greg has officially won. You may want to write this down. It's long. And case sensitive."

Minjee couldn't even get words out. She was waving at him now, trying to catch her breath. "I'm actually crying," she managed, half-laughing, half-sniffling.

James nodded, completely straight-faced. "As far as I'm concerned, you've earned every last penny."

Then he grinned at her. Open, pleased, and genuinely congratulatory. Like she'd pulled off the perfect heist.

Minjee put her hands over her ears. "No, no. I don't want to hear it. I won't have a reason to come back here if you tell it to me."

She saw James's eyes soften. And, just beneath that, sadness.

"Minjee," he said quietly. "In my letter... it's best if... no plans, no next–"

Minjee drew up everything she had. "Please. Do not try to get me to break up with you again." She kept her voice steady. Just barely. "I know this is our last planned visit. But just let me have this. Let me try to come back to you."

James rubbed a hand across his forehead, then dragged it down over his eyelids. Pressed his palm there like he could hold something back.

"Don't hurt your ganglion cells," Minjee said softly.

James let out a low, huffed laugh. "You are impossible." His hands dropped and he looked at her. His expression was equal parts fond and exasperated.

"Please. Just let me have this." She turned to look around. "Don't try to convince me not to visit. I already did the paperwork. And now you're in this..." She gestured vaguely at the plastic tables, the scuffed walls. "This glorious new space. What is this, a spa?"

James briefly shut his eyelids hard, like something behind them wanted out and he had to keep it locked in.

Then, with a practiced lightness, "This is a side of Lompoc that's a little more like a 'campus.' Rules are a little different here."

The visiting room was only half-full and half-loud. Families clung to each other in that bleary, polite way people do when they've run out of things to say but don't want to let go. Kids squirmed on laps. Plastic chairs squeaked.

Minjee glanced at the couple beside them, mid-forties or fifties maybe, seated shoulder to shoulder, quietly talking. The woman's head hovered close to the man's shoulder. Alarmingly close. Just a hair away from resting there.

She leaned in slightly, her voice low. "Can I sit next to you?"

James didn't nod, exactly. Just flicked his eyes toward the guards, then back to her.

No one was watching too closely.

She stood slowly, circled the table, and sat beside him.

No one objected.

For a moment, they didn't touch. Then, under the table, her hand–tentative, searching–found his. The first touch that was completely theirs. Not watched. Not monitored. Just for them.

He laced his fingers through hers without fumbling.

She let out a slow breath.

JAMES

Her hand was warm. Not just warm. It felt like *her*.

The temperature of her skin, the texture of her fingers, the way she gripped him. Not tight, not uncertain, just there. It was unbearable. And he never wanted to let go.

They had only ever been this close in motion. Kissing hello. Kissing goodbye.

But this was different. This was stillness. This was proximity. And it was harder than he expected. She was right there. Close enough to touch. Close enough to smell. He could feel the heat of her beside him. He could smell her. *Kumquats. Definitely kumquats.* It was all right there.

And all he could think was: *How am I supposed to walk away from this?*

She was the one who broke the silence. "I told my grand-mother about you," she said softly. "The one who taught me to cook."

James blinked. Her fingers were still threaded through his. Her thumb brushing his lightly.

His chest tightened. *Why?*

"She said if I have a boyfriend, I should tell my parents."

James tried not to react. He tried to keep his face still. But inside, something dropped.

You don't have to do that. You shouldn't have to. You shouldn't.

This was going to end. This was supposed to end.

And yet, her hand was still in his. Her voice still steady.

"So I told them," she continued. "Over the phone. Which is not a great way to tell my parents that my boyfriend is in prison."

She let out a breath, almost a laugh. "I told them about the letters."

James closed his eyes.

What are you doing? Why are you doing this to yourself?

She should be preparing to walk away. She should be packing this up as a beautiful mistake. Her epic failure.

He opened his eyes. Looked at her.

And there she was. So close. So tender.

Warm eyes full of strength. And clarity. And a kind of certainty he didn't know what to do with. The kind of look that didn't say *yours, comma,* but said *yours. Period.*

Minjee went on. "The terrible thing is that they were just... silent. I could almost imagine their faces. But I couldn't see them. So it was just silence. For a long time." She gave the smallest shrug. "My mom was more audibly upset. But my dad was calm. That's a bad sign. It means he isn't mad yet. He's thinking."

She paused, then added, with a small, bitter smile, "At the end of the call, he calmly suggested that this is a phase. Just for the summer. Just letters."

MINJEE

James listened for a long time. His jaw tensed ever so slightly as she spoke, though his breath stayed steady. Or maybe too steady.

They sat in silence after that.

Minjee looked down at his hand entwined with hers. Tanned fingers. Calloused. Rough in a way you didn't get from slicing hippocampi. But they held her with a sort of wisdom. A sort of purpose. Like she was something known. Something he couldn't let go of, no matter how many times he told her to walk away.

She ran her thumb across the back of his hand.

James spoke low and rumbly, almost to himself. "Just letters."

She looked up just as he looked down. Their eyes missed each other by a second.

"It was just letters," he said again.

Minjee didn't reply right away. She could still hear her father's voice. That slow, careful detachment. *It's just for the summer. Just letters.*

When she looked back, James was watching her. Unruffled. Composed, like always. But open in a way he rarely let himself be. "It's because it was letters," he said. He squeezed her hand. "That's how we got here."

Her brow furrowed slightly. She got it.

"If we'd met in the real world," she said quietly, "we might have seemed too different."

A small smile flickered at his mouth. "We would've stayed on the surface," he continued. "I would've tried to give you some Bitcoin though."

She smiled. "You would've tried to get me to visit your apartment."

James chuckled. "You would've never come. You already have a job."

They both laughed, quiet and knowing. The version of them that might've bumped into each other in the real world was almost funny now. A foolish shadow of who they really were.

She thought for a moment. "You wouldn't have told me about your mom. I wouldn't have told you about the church."

He nodded. "You wouldn't have called me Gatsby. I would've never called you Frodo."

She looked down at their hands again. "But with letters… there was nowhere to hide. Just words. Just the truth. One page at a time."

James was quiet for a moment. "Letters are slower."

She nodded. "Yeah. But they go deeper."

Their fingers stayed laced. Still no one came over. The visiting room hummed behind them. Quiet voices, vending machine hum, the distant clink of quarters.

"I don't think we would've gotten here any other way," she said.

James's hand tightened, just slightly, around hers.

"No," he said. "We wouldn't have."

JAMES

"I want to touch you so much more," she whispered. "Holding hands is already more than I thought we could have. But I was foolish. It just makes me want more."

James stared at her. Into her. He felt it too deeply.

Why was she saying these things out loud? Things he could barely let himself feel, let alone name. They were too heavy. Too much to exist under.

He said nothing. Didn't trust what might come out.

But she caught it. "What?"

He tried not to look startled.

"Why do you look like that?" she asked.

She could probably see right through him. Probably knew what was in his mind. What he had in mind.

They spoke at the same time–

She said, "You might not–"

He said, "There might be–"

They both stopped.

"What?" James asked.

"No, you," Minjee said, looking straight at him.

He paused. Should he say it? Should he do it?

"Do you trust me?"

That clearly wasn't the question she expected. But her answer came fast. Certain.

"Yes."

James didn't move quickly. He unthreaded his hand from hers. One stayed on top of the table, casual. The other slipped beneath.

There was a slit in her wrap dress. He'd noticed it when she walked.

He found her knee first. Bare skin, just above the bend.

She inhaled, a little startled, but didn't pull away.

His hand was steady. He traced upward, slowly, like he was reading her letters. Following each line. Taking his time.

"Is this..." he started.

"Yes," she whispered, already breathless. "Yes. It is."

In a low voice, he coached her. "You have to look away."

Minjee angled her face slightly to the side.

"Act like nothing's happening."

Her face twitched with the ghost of a smile. One eyebrow lifting in brief amusement, then relaxing into stillness.

Every inch forward was a question. Every pause, a chance to stop. She never stopped him. When he reached her, she gasped, just barely, but turned it into a cough.

Then her lips moved, barely audible. "I was wearing my bathing suit earlier..."

He didn't look at her. He was too close. Too focused.

But he could hear the smile in her voice. "And you said not to."

He felt the laugh catch in his throat, and for a second, they were both trying not to smile.

His hand steady on her, her breath becoming unsteady. "Unbelievable," he muttered.

He didn't look at her. Didn't move his head. He could feel her trying to stay still. Trying hard. Clearly struggling.

So he started to speak. Low. Steady. "Would it help," he murmured, "if I wrote you a letter now?"

She swallowed. Her eyes glassy. She gave a small nod.

"Dear Minjee," he said. "Let me tell you about life after the downfall. *The long con.*"

She was already smiling before he got to it.

"This guy named Greg started writing to me. A terrible scammer. But the letters... they were good. First, he said his name was Jessica. Then, he started calling himself Minjee, to feel a little more Korean."

She exhaled sharply–half a laugh, half a surrender–and tried to calm her face.

"The letters made me smile, even when I didn't want to. Maybe that was my mistake, keeping them tucked under my mattress like they meant something. He called me Gatsby. Replaced the jazz band with a DJ. West Egg became Western and Wilshire."

Minjee closed her eyes. Bit her lower lip. Took slow, steadying breaths.

"But Greg really sank his teeth in when he sent me a photo. Still, I kept fighting the con. Tried not to fall for it."

She glanced at him, just for a beat, before looking away. But it was enough. Her eyes were liquid. Her breath uneven.

"Shhh," James soothed, easing off for a moment, letting her recover. But only for a second.

He leaned in. Found his rhythm again. "Then you showed up."

Her head dropped slightly and her hands found his arm beneath the table. Gripping him, firm and urgent, like if she didn't hold on, she might fall apart right there. Never mind that he was the one pushing her over the edge.

He kept going. Voice rougher now, fraying at the edges. "I resisted for so long. But if I had to choose... If I could undo all the dumb things I did... If I could erase the rise and the fall... But this was the only way I ever got to you..."

He took a breath, steadying himself. "I'd do it all again."

He shouldn't have looked at her. But he did. And she looked back.

"For this," he said. "For one moment with you."

Minjee's lips parted, but only one word came out. "James."

She didn't cry out. Didn't shudder. Just a held breath. The faintest tremor in her body. And then the slow deepening of her inhale.

He stayed with her until her breathing settled. Her cheeks remained flushed. Her pupils still wide and dark. But, slowly, gently, he withdrew. Rested his hand on his knee.

Neither of them looked at the other.

But he was glad he'd told her. The only way he could.

MINJEE

She should've been spiraling.

What just happened?

Did we just–?

Did he just–?

Did I just–?

But no real questions were forming. Her mind was all sensation and breath and heat and silence. Like her body hadn't caught back up to time yet. She just sat there, weightless, trying to catch up to herself.

To what he'd done. To what he'd said.

Not just the touch. Not just the way he touched her. But the words. The way he said them. Like it was one of his lives. Like a letter. Like he needed her to know something without saying it outright. Like the con had turned on itself.

It was all of it. His hands, his words, his voice. Together, they folded into something she couldn't untangle. Something that left her breathless.

They had touched so rarely. Five kisses. One handhold. And now, this.

She was still floating in it, barely able to think straight. But she turned to him anyway, trying desperately to act normal. To sound like a woman whose body hadn't just come undone in a prison visitation room. Like she wasn't still shaped around his hand. Like her heart wasn't bucking wildly against her ribs.

"This can't be our last visit," she said.

James blinked, slow and unsure, like he was still catching up to her words.

"I don't know how yet," she went on. "But I'm going to come back. Maybe Thanksgiving. Maybe sometime in the fall."

He didn't say anything at first. His face was neutral. Careful.

Then finally, he sighed, just a little, and said. "That would be... nice."

Not a yes. Not even a maybe. But she'd told him before: *Just let me have this.*

So he didn't argue. Didn't correct her. Didn't stop her from making plans.

She knew, somewhere inside her, that he wasn't agreeing. That he was just letting her pretend. But she couldn't help herself. She kept grasping.

"I'll borrow Rosalie's car," she said, too quickly. "There are people I know in Santa Barbara now..."

Her voice softened. Hopeful. Trying.

"They let you bring food in here. I saw people." She gestured vaguely at the other visitors, hunting for proof, for precedent. "So you can try my brown butter–"

She stopped. Froze. Then flushed. Deep and fast.

"Oh God."

She covered her mouth, mortified. But also to hide the smile tugging at the corner of her lips. Because she could feel it. Laughter blooming under the horror, rising like a bubble she couldn't suppress.

He had definitely touched it now.

And she couldn't unhear it. *Brown butter cornbread.* Her brain refused to move on. Which only made it worse. So much worse. And so much funnier.

She snuck a glance at him. That was a mistake. Because they both saw it at once. Because now she knew *he* knew. And he *knew* that she knew.

"NO!" she gasped, truly gasped.

He was holding his lips tight, jaw trembling with restraint, his cheekbones sharp with the effort of keeping it in.

Then it broke. A brilliant, toothy smile cracked across his face like a dam giving way. Pure mischief, radiant and soundless laughter, bright and wordless understanding.

He knew. He *so* knew.

She could almost see it. The word "cornbread" blinking across his face like a neon sign.

And then he lost it. Laughter burst out of him, full and unrestrained. He threw his head back, breathless, shoulders shaking. Totally gone. No hope of composure.

And now she was laughing too. Hard. Her stomach hurt. Her face was on fire. She couldn't stop.

"Please stop thinking it," she begged, gripping her burning cheeks.

"I have no idea what you're talking about," he managed–so terrible at playing innocent, still laughing, barely able to breathe.

"I *know* what you're thinking! Stop thinking about it!" she swatted at him, still giggling uncontrollably.

They both turned away from each other, trying to stop, shoulders shaking. Trying so hard.

But they were *definitely* both thinking about her brown butter cornbread.

JAMES

His abs actually hurt. His face hurt. He rubbed his jaw, trying to pull himself together. But he could still hear it–her laugh, wild and warm and completely undone.

Then came the buzz. The loud clicks. The metallic clatter of the visitor door.

There it was.

Minjee was leaving. James had been trying to prepare for this moment. Prepare her. Prepare himself.

He'd said everything he could say. He'd done everything he could do. Held nothing back. Let her have everything.

He was supposed to be ready. Ready to let go. Ready to carry no regrets.

But Minjee stood close. Not touching him. And he wasn't ready.

She tilted her face toward his, her voice barely a breath against his chin. "This isn't the end, right? I'll visit again."

What does he do? Does he tell her the truth? Or does he give her what she wants? What she needs?

"I'd like that," he said simply.

Then his hands found her shoulders. Steady. Careful. This, at least, he could do with clarity.

He returned to discipline. To boundaries. Because he couldn't do what he wanted to do. He couldn't breach every line. Couldn't pull her in and press every inch of himself to her. If he did, if he let himself get that close, he might never be able to stop.

He kissed her. Held her by the shoulders and kissed her. But his mouth moved like it was the last time. Because it was. He kissed her like it was the end. Not just the end of life six, but the end of a life with breath, with taste, with color. With kumquats. With brown butter cornbread. With letters.

He'd poured so much of himself into those letters. But thankfully, the form was measured. Contemplated. Controlled. But this kiss. It was the opposite. He tried to keep it measured. Disciplined. Tried to keep some part of himself separate from her. But the form betrayed him. He tried, *truly* tried, to kiss her like he could hold the line. To stay just far enough.

But at the end of the kiss, she shifted. A soft shrug. A sleight of hand. And then, somehow, she was folded into him. Tucked in. Anchored.

His arms were around her. And hers were around him. Not with heat, but with quiet finality. Her body pressed gently, completely, into his. She gave herself over to the moment. To him. And he couldn't stop her. Couldn't stop himself. She was everything he wasn't allowed to have. To want. To need.

He felt every part of her. The full weight and shape of her against his chest. She didn't say it. But he felt it anyway: *Don't deny it. Don't deny me. Yours. Minjee.*

There was no way around it.

She must have felt him too. All the ways he wanted her. All the ways he would never have her.

Lompoc/Los Angeles - 2012

39.

Dear Minjee,

By the time you read this, I'll be gone. Not from the world or anything dramatic. Just from here. From Lompoc.

I didn't tell you during the visit.

Maybe it was because I'm a thoughtful guy who didn't want to ruin the day. That would be partly true.

Maybe it was because I'm a coward who couldn't watch your face change when you realized what this meant. That's more true.

But mostly it was because I'm a dumbass who couldn't figure out how to explain something like this without it sounding like an ending. And I didn't want it to end like that.

Here's what I know: I've been selected for voluntary deportation through some diplomatic program. A prison population solution dressed up as a homecoming. Non-violent, low-level offenders agreeing to early release in exchange for permanent removal. Highly competitive I'm told. Just like Williams.

The alternative was being held for a brief eternity in ICE detention. Likely in Arizona. Months in legal limbo with no guarantee of mail, movement, or decency. Same outcome, just slower. And meaner.

So I chose exile. Signed up for it.

They don't tell you when, just that it's soon. Just the decision, then silence. That's why they moved me to the camp. The soft launch. Kicking me out of the country with the softest boots imaginable.

I didn't want our final visit to be filled with the weight of this. I just kept thinking: Let her have this. Let's hold hands. Let's laugh until we're crying. Let it be good. For her. Let her walk away with good memories.

Maybe that was wrong. Maybe you'll hate me for it. Maybe it was just cruelty disguised as mercy... letting you leave with hope.

If I caused you pain, I'm sorry. If it helps, I feel it too.

I don't know when I'll be able to write again. Could be months. Might be longer. The truth is, I'm stepping into a tunnel. Made of paperwork and policy. No forwarding address. No clear exit.

So this is the last letter. For now.

But maybe, there's a version of this story where you come to Korea one day. Maybe you've lived a few more lives. Maybe you've mastered mandoo pan-fried in lard. And maybe, you decide to visit. To look for a church. To look for an open door. To look for something.

Maybe I'll be there. Maybe I'll be looking too. Maybe I'll cook for you. You can even touch my dduk. (Double entendre fully intended.)

Until then.
Yours,
James

Part 5

Seoul

Present Day

The television was still on when he came into the room, casting flickers of light across the bedroom. Some over-the-top reality cooking competition rumbled on. Tonight's drama centered on a Korean-American chef from Kentucky, who had pulled ahead by producing a single, molecular gastronomic miracle of a ravioli that tasted like *bibimbap*. Complete with a runny egg yolk inside. He pointed the remote and the television went silent.

She had fallen asleep watching, like always. She was a terrible bed hog. Always had been.

She was curled up on top of all the blankets, arms splayed across a stack of papers. He leaned down to tug them free and caught a glimpse of the title: "MDMA Self-Administration in Rats…" And on the other side of her wrist, it continued: "…Serotonin Transporters."

He set the papers aside and laughed quietly to himself. *Of course.* Leave it to Minjee. Working on a pharma pitch deck about rats on molly, like she was trying to troll all their past lives at once.

He slid in behind her, careful not to wake her. Within seconds, she shifted–slowly, then decisively–into his space. Half her face now rested on his pillow.

He smiled, amused, and nudged her gently. "Hey," he whispered. "Scoot."

She grumbled softly and turned away from him, settling onto her own pillow. Then mumbled something he didn't catch.

He leaned in, lips near her ear, his chest pressing gently on her back. "What?" he asked, voice low.

She shifted again, just enough to murmur, "Waiting for you."

He laughed softly. Of course she would put it that way. He never got tired of her like this. Half-drowsy, a little bossy, entirely sweet. Fully his.

The apartment was warm. One of the city's summer nights where even the AC struggled to keep up. They kept it just cool enough to sleep.

She wore her lightest pajamas: a pink tank top and matching shorts. The silky kind, soft with stretch. Faint hearts and polka dots scattered across the fabric.

His eyes moved over her, finger-light, taking her in slowly. Her back curved, one shoulder bare. The way the fabric hugged her, just at the slope of her waist, made him want to touch her. Not out of hunger, exactly. Though there was that, too. Something slower.

His hand slipped under the waistband of her shorts, fingertips brushing the edge of her hip bone, then lower. Soft. Sure.

She sighed. "Mmm... what a good dream..." she whispered, eyes still closed.

He kissed the back of her neck.

She reached down without looking, tugging the shorts over her hips as she nuzzled closer, like she was finding her place against him. His shirt came off easily. Quietly.

They didn't say much. They didn't need to.

They folded into each other like a familiar craving. Slow. Certain. Already satisfying.

Lompoc FCI - August 27, 2012

J ames was walking past admin when he heard it, "Shin."
He turned.

Sam was leaning in his office doorway, one hand holding
a ceramic mug, the other tapping a pen against his leg.
"You've got a visitor tomorrow."

James blinked. "What?"

"And," Sam added, like he wasn't sure how casually to say
it, "you're shipping out in forty-eight hours."

James stared at him. Sam waited. Sipped his coffee. "I
know. It's a lot for a Monday."

James cleared his throat. "Who scheduled the visit?"

Sam paused, just for a beat. James saw the way his eyes
sharpened, just a flicker. Not quite a question. But something.

He tapped the pen once, then turned and disappeared
into his office. A moment later, he reappeared with a clip-
board.

"Tuesdays are light," he said. "Wasn't hard to get you a
slot." He scanned the form. "Jessica Cooper."

Jessica. Cooper.

It took a second for his brain to catch up.

Jessica Minjee Cooper.

The name from her first letter. The name on her ID. The
name she didn't use with him anymore, not really. Not in

letters. Not in his head. She hadn't been Jessica Cooper in a long time.

Minjee. She was visiting him. Tomorrow. The day before he shipped out to Korea.

His heart–already shattered, swept into a box, sealed and labeled "fragile" and "irrelevant"–started to shake. Not in grief. Not in panic. Just... movement. Like all the broken pieces had started vibrating again.

But all he managed to say was, "Jessica Cooper?"

Sam looked up. Eyebrow raised. Not in judgment. More like he was watching a machine glitch for the first time.

"That name mean something to you?"

James didn't move. Didn't breathe.

He steadied himself. Tried to ignore the weird sensation of his body rebooting in pieces. Like his organs were all zombies trying to claw their way out.

He blinked. Opened his eyes wider. Maybe that would help.

"Uh... I'll be there."

Sam stuck out his chin, nodded once.

James turned to go.

He'd made it halfway down the hall when Sam called after him, casual as ever, "You don't have questions about the whole *deportation* thing?"

Lompoc FCI - August 28, 2012

MINJEE

S he should have brought a book.

The waiting room at Lompoc was taking its sweet time. All the visitors had been checked in. And now they were waiting. Together. Under flickering fluorescent lights. On cheap plastic chairs. In a box of a building.

But actually, no. The wait was good. She needed the time. Even after over two hours on the road. In silence. No podcasts. No playlists. No calls. Minjee never drove in LA if she could help it. But it was good for her. Just her, the wheel, and that low repetitive chant in the back of her head: *what are you doing what are you doing what are you doing.*

She wasn't sure she had an answer yet.

She adjusted the flutter sleeve of her off-white maxi dress. Navy blue polka-hearts. Soft cotton. Layered. Comfortable. A dress you could wear anywhere, to do anything: eat dinner, take a nap, or visit a prison.

She'd tried to look nice. Pretty, if she could help it. It was part of their private fiction. That these institutional visits were dates.

The packet of brown butter cornbread sat next to her, wrapped in foil. It wasn't piping hot anymore. It was best eaten straight from the cast iron. With whipped honey butter. But they weren't going to let her bring a cast iron into Lompoc. Not even into the camp part.

Her face flushed slightly. God, that line.

Touch my brown butter cornbread.

She hadn't even meant it that way. Until he did. And then... he did.

She'd never been particularly... adventurous. Not like that. Not in public. The most risky thing she'd done before James was making out in a parked car on a dark cul-de-sac when she was a junior in high school.

But this was different. James was different.

She swallowed and glanced around, suddenly self-conscious. As if the other visitors might somehow see what she was remembering. He had traced her like the last page of a book he wasn't allowed to keep. Traced her like he was writing a letter.

She squeezed her thighs together under the layers of her dress. She couldn't think about the way he hadn't rushed. The way he seemed to know exactly where to go. The way it felt.

She closed her eyes. She still had no plan. No script. What was this visit? Just a goodbye? Just closure? What was she doing here?

She didn't know what she was going to say. Only that being here was already saying something. Only that they weren't finished.

The door buzzed.

The other visitors started to move. Gathering children, standing slowly, following the rhythm like they had done it a hundred times before. Minjee followed them in.

And there he was. Standing near the back of the room, hands in his pockets. He looked different. Not bad. Just... less buttoned-up. His hair was a little longer than usual. A little wilder. He hadn't shaved. There were faint shadows under his eyes.

And something else. A flicker behind his gaze. Uncontained.

She realized–he usually cleaned up for her. Usually came in sharp, composed, whole. But today he looked raw. Like she'd caught him off guard. Like he hadn't slept in days and was thinking too fast to speak. Like he was on fire. Or starved.

Her chest ached.

For a moment, she thought he looked angry. But it wasn't anger. It was something more dangerous.

Then his eyes found hers. And even from that distance, something changed. His body went still but not quiet. There was a vibration in it. Low and taut. Like a wire pulled too tight, too hard. Waiting to snap.

She didn't wave. Didn't smile. She walked toward him with quick, steady steps, her shoulders squaring with each one. Maybe a little too fast. Maybe not fast enough.

He stepped forward. One step. Two.

And when they met, she didn't say anything. She just reached for him. Both hands to his face. Fingertips along his jaw, rough with stubble. She pulled him in and kissed him. Not playfully, not softly. Hard. *Punishing.*

She didn't even realize how mad she was. Not until her mouth found his. Not until the kiss lit the match. Mad that he was leaving. Mad that this was the end. Mad that he hadn't told her. Mad that he had the nerve to matter this much.

She kissed him like it was the only language she had left. Like she was throwing every truth in his face, every line hurled at him. Her mouth, hands, body–all of her indicting him.

She pressed herself into him. Fully, deliberately. Every soft part of her aligned with every hard line of him.

You think you get to walk away from this? You think you get to leave?

This wasn't a dare. It wasn't want. It was punishment.

And he took it. He didn't resist. Didn't stop her.

He kissed her like a man who knew he deserved it. All of it. Every ounce of her fury, her ache, her need to make him pay. His mouth opened under hers, rough and surrendered, letting her pour all of it into him. His arms locked around her, hard and possessive, like he needed to be held accountable by the force of her. So he couldn't flinch. So he couldn't run. His hands splayed across her back, dragging her closer. Tighter. Like he wanted to absorb every part of her rage, down to the fire in her bones.

But he needed her to feel him, too. She could feel it in the grip of his fingers, the tension in his chest, the way his body folded around hers like a vow. Like he was pouring regret into every corner of her. Like the bear hug of sorry.

He moved against her like he wanted it to hurt him. Like he needed it to. Maybe that was the point. To leave with her burned onto his skin. To carry the scar in his mouth.

She felt him pull her all the way in, clasping her against him like it was the only move he had left. If he couldn't keep her, he could at least be ruined by her.

It wasn't sweet. It wasn't slow.

It was the kind of kiss that says: *Now. Take it now. While there's still time.*

And he did.

She could feel it in the way he kissed her back. Like he understood. Like he knew the sentence was already written. Like he wanted to go down with her name on his tongue.

JAMES

He sat. First into the closest seat, then slid awkwardly to the next one to make room for her. *Okay.* So this is what Min-jee looks like right before she kills you.

Her face was basically neutral. If someone had asked him to point out how he knew she was angry, he'd come up short. A slight tension in her brow. A glare, but barely. It was like watching someone prepare for a silent, efficient assassination. He felt fairly certain someone, perhaps a pen pal of hers, was going to get murdered here today. In the visitation room of a federal facility.

She sat. Wordlessly. And she was... hot.

Yes, *hot* in that sense. He always thought she was hot. Lips plush and a little swollen, cheeks flushed, one of her sweet dresses hugging her frame just enough that, yeah, he could absolutely imagine undressing her right here, even now. Especially after that goofy-ass polo shirt. That was just part of his personality now.

But also, she was hot like she was radiating heat. Like there was a fire happening at their disgusting plastic four-top, and the chairs were bolted down so he couldn't quite escape the flames. His eyebrows were going to get singed.

She just stared. Unblinking. Then calmly, clearly, with the kind of quiet conviction that gets you buried under a parking lot, "Fuck you."

She closed her eyes. Took a breath.

Okay. That tracks. He nodded slightly. The kind of nod that says, *Yup. Yup yup yup.*

That is definitely the energy she had kissed–

"I want to–"

She stopped. Hard. Eyes still closed.

Wait. Did she mean... she wanted to... well. That changed things.

Did it? That was *also* the energy she had kissed–

And then, completely uninvited, a line drawing popped into his head. From <u>A Wrinkle in Time</u>. *Oh God. Why now.* A picture of a string, initially stretched between two points, the ends brought together by a pair of hands so an ant could cross from one side to the other. A wrinkle in time. One of the only illustrations in the book.

He tried to shut it down, but he was experiencing what could only be called... delight. Which was, objectively, the worst possible emotion right now.

He screwed his lips together, trying to hold it in. But she caught it. Her eyes locked on him like a sniper lining up a shot.

Oh. Okay. She could be even angrier. Apparently murder was not her final level. Good to know.

Any hint of a smile was instantly erased from his face. But not fast enough.

The look she gave him was pure contempt wrapped in confusion. Maybe he wasn't going to be murdered. At least not in the next sixty seconds.

"What," she said. One word. Contextually a question, but emotionally a threat.

He tried to straighten his face. "Nothing."

"Are you... amused?"

Ah. Murder was back on the table.

"No! Not amused." He tried for innocent. Failed. He furrowed his brow. "I had an... inappropriate thought."

Her eyebrows shot skyward. Appalled. Incredulous. Like she could not believe what she was hearing. Like he'd just whispered a pickup line during a baptism. Or proposed to go down on her during a eulogy. Or offered her an orgasm (another one) right there between vending machines and COs.

"No, not inappropriate like that. Just... not appropriate for this situation. Like it doesn't fit. It doesn't be–"

"So you mean the literal definition of 'inappropriate,'" she said flatly.

"Yes. Exactly. It was just a funny image. Not funny-ha-ha, but funny like–"

Oh God. He was rambling. He never rambled. He must be really uncomfortable. Which made sense. One probably gets uncomfortable right before being murdered.

"It's from <u>A Wrinkle in Time</u>."

Wow. That was a lot of contempt. So much contempt on such a beautiful face. Impressive, really.

"I mean, you know the string picture? With the ant? When they're explaining–"

"Of course I know that picture. Everyone knows that picture. If you say 'the picture from <u>A Wrinkle in Time</u>,' that is the picture."

Okay. Exasperated now. But the anger was still burning behind her eyes. He had to do better.

"Well... it's because you said, you know, 'Fuck you.' And I thought, yeah, that makes sense. And then you said 'I want to–' and even though that totally changes the meaning of 'fuck you,' I just thought, yeah, that makes sense too."

She closed her eyes. Her eyeballs were twitching beneath the lids. That probably wasn't a good sign.

"It was like... one end of 'fuck you' meant, you know, 'fuck you,' and the other end meant... something else. And then the string got brought together, like in the book... so both ends were right next to each other. Same words. But now they're basically touching. Totally different–"

She held up a hand. He stopped.

She pressed both palms to her eyes. Exhaled.

"Are you seriously using a literary reference... from a goddamn children's book... to suggest that I both want to..."

She searched for the right phrasing. Took a breath.

"'Violently mess you up' and–"

She paused. Maybe searching again. Her eyes still completely covered. Maybe she was looking for... something less graphic. Maybe less true.

He nodded, too fast. Trying to be helpful. Encouraging. Like this was some kind of collaborative fill-in-the-blank.

"And... 'violently mess me up'?"

God. That was not the move. He should stop. He needed to stop. Why couldn't he stop? Was this what happened when he had no emotional guard left? Just panic and raw, open yearning?

And then, to his complete and utter horror, she burst out laughing.

That laugh. Full-body. Clapping. The one from the photo. The one that almost killed him. *Ah.* So this was how she was going to do it.

"Oh my God!" she gasped.

He couldn't help it. He smiled. Relief and joy and something close to disbelief.

Delight.

She was still pissed. But she was laughing. And he was still going to die. But at least now it would be from her.

MINJEE

He was grinning at her. Big. Open. A little stupid. Relieved, like someone who had just been told they weren't going to die today.

And honestly? It was kind of grounding.

Something about how unguarded it was. Like his whole face had opened up and surrendered to hand her a clear shot to his soul.

She wanted to stay mad. She really wanted to. But instead, as the laughter died in her throat, she felt it slipping away. That sharp edge. That righteous heat.

So she gave up with a sigh. Reluctant, almost annoyed at herself. *Fine.* She wouldn't be mad. But she was a little pissed she didn't get to be mad.

And then she saw it. The brown butter cornbread wrapped in foil, patiently waiting at the edge of the table.

She slid it across her body so that it stopped gently in front of him. Then dropped her arms onto the tabletop and folded them, burying her face in a makeshift tent of shame and emotional triage.

"I brought you something," she muttered. Her voice was muffled. "It's better straight out of the oven. It's not that good right now."

She sighed. Then, sharper, "But you can't say it. You are not allowed to say the words."

Her arms tightened. A fortress of forearms. There was anger in her voice again. Protective, preemptive anger.

She couldn't look at him. But she knew. She just *knew.*

"Do. Not. Say it."

A beat.

"I'm serious."

A pause. Then his voice, tentative, "...Can I... touch it?"

To her great displeasure, she cracked, just a little. A rueful smile pulled at her mouth as she tilted her head, just enough to peer out from under the shield.

"I truly hate that I ever wrote those words."

James leaned in, mock-serious. "I'm a big fan of consent. Huge. Enthusiastic consent. I would never touch–"

"DO NOT, JAMES JUWON SHIN."

As he started opening the aluminum, she realized, with utter and complete mortification, that she could not watch him. *Oh no.* She knew what he was going to say right as he...

"So I can eat your–"

She buried her face back in the tent as she cut his words short. "I should not have brought it. That's my own fault. I did not think this through."

She heard the crinkle of foil as he started unwrapping it.

Then, "Fuuuck. It's warm."

Oh God. Her soul left her body.

She stayed hidden in the crook of her arms, refusing to lift her head. Maybe if she stayed there long enough, she'd die. Or disappear. Or rewind time and *not* bring him the world's most inappropriate baked good.

A beat of silence. Then a soft, throaty noise–was that a moan?

She squeezed her eyes shut. *Please, for the love of God.* Don't let him moan over the cornbread.

"This is..." he said, his voice low and reverent, "...so moist."

She kicked him under the table.

He didn't stop. "The edges have a little crunch," he murmured, like he was narrating porn for artisanal bakers, "but the middle's just... impossibly soft." He gave a low whistle. "It like gives a little when you press into it."

She made a sound. Somewhere between a scream and a prayer.

"The butter," he said, chewing thoughtfully. "It tastes... it's nutty. And salty. And sweet. Like... layered. Complex."

She gritted her teeth.

"I can't stop tasting it," he growled. "I keep going back. Just to make sure."

Yep. Dying. Definitely dying inside.

He paused, just long enough for her to think maybe, mercifully, he was done.

Then, "It coats your whole mouth, you know? Just lingers there. Slow and... buttery."

She let out a strangled noise and slammed her forehead against her arms.

"Are you blushing?" he asked, far too innocently. "I'm just eating. You're the one with the dirty mind."

A beat.

His voice dropped. "I just want to *savor* it."

He went quiet. Finally.

She stayed buried in the crook of her arms for a few more seconds, just in case. Then, cautiously, she lifted her head.

He wasn't looking at her. Just staring off to the side, still chewing, leaned back in his chair like he had nowhere else to be. Was his leg up on the opposite seat? When did that happen? And, of course, he was licking his fingers. Slowly. Absent-mindedly. He seemed unaware she was watching.

It wasn't to tease her. Which somehow made it worse. Because it was definitely doing something to her. He was just... enjoying it. Enjoying her cornbread. Like it was the best thing he'd eaten in a year. Maybe the best thing he'd put in his mouth. Ever.

Her eyes narrowed. Her heart kicked. *Un. Be. Lievable.*

JAMES

That brown butter cornbread really was... something else. Warm. Lingering. He could taste it on the back of his tongue. Salted, buttery, just a little sweet. It had depth. Character. Like it knew exactly what it was doing.

He lounged in that uncomfortable plastic chair, licking the caramelized butter from his fingers, letting the taste settle in his mouth so he could just sit still and recover. And that's when he felt it.

Not the cornbread. Not even her voice. Just... presence. She was looking at him. He could feel it. Sharpened and precise. Like the point of a blade pressed flat against his skin. Surgical. Cutting straight through the side of his face.

He turned.

She was out of the tent now. Elbows still on the table, hands folded loosely in front of her. Calm. Composed. Chilling.

And, under the surface, something else. Something honed. Reckless in intention, but not in aim. A controlled kind of chaos. Something he recognized.

Oh. Oh, shit.

She wasn't mad anymore. She was done being mad. She was going to even the score. She was going to make him regret everything.

She didn't say anything. Not right away. Just tilted her head slightly and whispered, under her breath, almost too softly to hear, "You wanna play?"

And he instantly thought: *no no no no no no no.*

And then her hand moved under the table.

He froze.

Because he knew exactly what she was about to do. And it wasn't like last time. The sweet, firm hand-holding. The romance of interlaced fingers. The delicate brush of a thumb.

No. This was not that.

This was *fuck you* energy. And also, just: *fuck you.*

The kind that said: *I'm going to make you sorry. Very sorry. Like your pants are going to feel sorry.*

Her fingers reached him. Confident, unhurried, devastating. He exhaled sharply, eyes darting around the visitation room. But no one was looking. No one cared. Apparently, the guards still didn't monitor under-table contact. Apparently, these were the ways to disappear in plain sight.

His whole body went still. Like he'd been hit. Or claimed.

Her hand. Firm. Just once. Just enough to make him feel how easy it would be to ruin him.

And then she leaned forward, lips barely parted, not smiling. "Savor that."

He did. Every part of him did. He sat there, aching. Uncomfortable. But not unfamiliar.

This, he knew. This, he could deal with. He woke up like this. Over and over. To the image of her in pearls and an apron. To the curve of her bikini beneath a damp yellow polo shirt. To her light finger, tracing his arm. To that one line, "*I want it. Bad.*" Played on loop by his double-crossing brain.

He shifted slightly in his seat. Winced. Let the ache settle where it needed to settle. The discomfort. The humiliation. It was hers. She gave it to him. And he took it.

And then he heard himself say it. Or confess it, rather. "The cornbread," he murmured, just loud enough for her to hear, "was totally worth it."

She blinked. Just once. And even though she was trying—so hard, so terribly hard—not to feel it, he saw it.

Pride.

For a second, something in her softened.

And then, it was gone. She shifted. Not much, just enough. A small change in angle and with it, a shift in intent.

And he felt it. Her hand moved again. Deliberate now. No longer just a warning shot.

He inhaled sharply. Because she was relentless. Not tender, not playful. Purposeful.

And not for his pleasure. Oh no, this wasn't about pleasure. This was the *fuck you* part. The part she had promised without saying it. The part he knew was coming the second she looked at him with that terrifying composure.

She was playing now. And he was the game.

This wasn't sweet. It wasn't slow. It was punishment.

And the worst part? He still wanted it. He still wanted her. Every devastating second.

He pressed the heel of his hand against the table—trying to stay still, to breathe evenly, to not completely lose his mind. Not just from the effort of keeping still, but from the dawning, unignorable reality that if she didn't stop, there were going to be... consequences.

Visible. Violent. Messy.

So he said the only thing that popped into his head. The only thing that might interrupt her vengeance before things got... untenable.

"I told you," he whispered, barely audible. "You already won, Greg."

Her hand froze.

He didn't look at her. Couldn't. He just stared straight ahead, jaw tight, chest rising and falling in quiet, controlled panic.

Then–coolly, almost casually–she said, "Oh. So you don't want me to... finish?"

He squinted. Not at her. At the air. Just trying to breathe.

But also... contemplating. Did he want her to finish? The honest answer? Of course he did. Desperately. Pathetically.

But also... no. She absolutely could not do this here. Not unless they were both prepared for federal-level consequences.

He closed his eyes. Exhaled. And then, as evenly as he could manage, "A mess. My pants. They would know."

A pause.

Then her voice, light and lethal, "Ah. You mean I would violently mess you up."

He opened one eye. A flicker of dread.

She was smiling now. Polite. Inevitable. Sugar-coated danger. "Like <u>A Wrinkle in Time</u>."

Then she did something strange. Totally unexpected.

She shifted in her seat. Wiggled, just slightly, like she was trying to get comfortable. She looked... awkward. Focused. A touch frustrated. Like something wasn't cooperating. Then she leaned forward.

No. She leaned down. All the way down, toward her ankles.

He blinked. *Are you tying your shoe? Looking for something? Planning your escape?*

She fumbled with something in her hand. And for a second, he caught a glimpse.

Nude-colored underwear. Seamless. Practical. The kind you pick up at the Gap in a three-pack without thinking too hard about it.

Not lacy. Not sheer. Not even black. Just... beige.

Not sexy. Well, not intended to be sexy. But right then, James decided: sexy is a term with range.

An everyday functional item. Thin and simple. Meant for comfort, not seduction.

And James could barely breathe.

MINJEE

Her panties were caught on one of her shoes. It was not elegant. Definitely not smooth.

If she had planned this out, she might have handled it differently. But she hadn't. Obviously. Because who plans to have sex in a federal prison visitation room? That would definitely take planning. Logistics. Forethought. But she hadn't. Not at all.

And yet... here she was. Crouched halfway under the table, wrestling with the sole of her shoe, which was stubbornly looped through her own underwear.

Tsk. Shoes first. Then underwear. That would've been a plan.

The fabric snagged again. She twisted awkwardly, trying not to flash the room or fall out of her chair. She finally tugged them free. Progress.

She balled them up in one hand. Thank God this dress had pockets. All her favorites did. She slipped them into one side, clean and easy, then looked up just in time to catch him watching.

James was not breathing.

"Hey." She waved a hand in front of his face.

He blinked. "What are you doing?"

She sighed. *Honestly.* Did she really have to explain everything?

He held up one hand. "I'm sorry. Did you just put some underwear into your pocket?"

"Yes," she said. A little too defensively.

His jaw tightened. He fidgeted. "Like you just have a pair of panties... loose. In your pocket?"

"Well," she said, as if it should be obvious, "I don't want you to make a mess."

And that was it. She saw it happen. The gears in his brain, which had briefly locked up from shock or blood loss or both, started grinding back to life. He blinked. Swallowed. Started breathing again, but not well.

"I don't think we should," he said.

That stung a little. She flinched, just slightly. "You don't want to?"

"No, it's not–" Too fast. Too loud. He tried again. Softer. Slower. "I mean. Yes. Of course I want to. I want to. I *definitely* want to."

"Then–" she offered, leaving the end of the sentence open.

"But not like this."

He looked down at the table. There was a scratch in the laminate plastic. One little groove, a little deeper than the rest. Of all the marks on this sad, bolted-down, excuse for a table, he'd picked that one to pour all his attention into.

He closed his eyes. Like it hurt.

"Minjee," he said. And even though it was just her name, it felt like an apology. "I want to have you. In whatever way you'll let me. I've got... ideas. A lot of them. Enough to go for hours. For days. For years. No amount of time would be enough. But not here. Not like this."

He opened his eyes again and tried to fix his face. To smooth away the ache. Just enough to show her he wasn't pulling away.

"You don't have to do this."

She looked down too. At the same scratch. Like that little groove was the only thing that mattered between them.

She reached out. Touched it lightly with one finger. "You're either very good at this game," she said, "or you haven't caught on yet."

He looked up, brows pulled in slightly. Just listening.

"Classic James!" She gave a dry little laugh. "You say all the right things. Just enough respect. Just enough soft eyes.

That's how you con me into giving you exactly what you want."

Now he looked startled. Genuinely confused.

And that's when she felt it. The clarity. The thing that had been there this whole time.

"You always do this," she said, with a quiet vehemence. "You tell me not to call you my boyfriend. So I call you my boyfriend. You say not to visit. So, of course, I visit. You say don't write. So I write."

She tilted her head, the edge finally gone from her voice. Something gentle, for the first time all visit.

"Don't you know me yet?"

JAMES

Wordlessly Minjee gestured for him to flip down the top of his pants.

James blinked, incredulous. What was happening?

He was already hanging on by a thread. There was so much coiled up in him. The cornbread (the actual cornbread). The loose underwear, like an emotional grenade hidden in her pocket. A Wrinkle in Time. The punishing kiss. The merciless touch. Her anger. Her want. All of it had stacked inside him like a spring-loaded mousetrap.

And now she was just... gesturing? Like this was the next logical step?

"And what if I refuse?" he asked, with a boldness that surprised him. A boldness he immediately wanted to kick his own ass for. Because, *really buddy? Refuse?*

He had been in prison for over a year. The beautiful girl, literally from his dreams, was practically asking to sit on his lap. And he was... what? Negotiating?

She gave him a look. Precise. Terrifying.

Oh no. This wasn't murder.

"You won't refuse," she said, flatly. "The narrative has been established."

Okay. That should not be hot.

James was learning a lot about himself today. His unexpected preference for seamless beige briefs. His enthusiasm for opening with cornbread. His vulnerability to petite pen pals who do not take no for an answer.

The way she was just... letting him know. That his fate had already been decided. And she would be very, very efficient about it.

This was not normal. He shouldn't be turned on by this. He really shouldn't.

Minjee reached over and covered his lap with her long skirt. Tiny navy blue hearts. Of course.

"Just a little," she whispered.

James ran both hands over his face. Because he knew himself. And he knew this was a terrible idea.

Why am I subjecting myself to this?

Because Minjee took off her panties and put them in her pocket. Because she told you to lower your waistband. Because tomorrow you're getting deported and you will never forgive yourself if you don't do this. Because there is no universe in which you turn this down.

So he does. He shifts slightly, breath held, and lowers the waistband just enough. Just a little, like she told him to.

And she slips onto his lap. Quietly. Casually. Like this is the most ordinary thing in the world.

He bites his lip to stifle a groan. Because. *Because.* The warmth of her. The weight of her. The way she fits against him. And it's all he can do, not to let go.

Not from lust, exactly. Though, that too. But from the fullness of it.

From ink on bureaucratic paper to warm kumquat-scented skin. From an imagined voice to the impossible nearness of her breathing. From signing *Yours*, to meaning it. With her body. With everything. From feeling like some has-been Jay Gatsby with a record to watching her choose this. *Him.* Now. In this terrible chair, under this bolted-down table.

Like she had read the whole story. And still turned the page.

She moves. Just slightly. Not even a roll of her hips. Just the suggestion of motion. And it's too much. It's everything.

He presses his lips together and simply exhales. Long. Slow. Shaking.

And she feels it. She knows.

MINJEE

Minjee was sitting in her own chair now. Back where she started. Knees together. Hands folded in her lap like nothing had happened. Nothing that could be definitively proven in federal proceedings.

There was probably... evidence. She could feel it. But thank God this dress had layers. She would just have to stand carefully when the visit ended. But nothing that couldn't be handled. Managed.

She glanced beside her.

James hadn't moved. Like someone trying to pretend nothing had just happened while his nervous system quietly rebooted. She could give him that.

His mouth was slightly open. His pupils were dilated. He'd probably had sex in better places. With more freedom. More movement. More noise. But the way he looked, like he'd hit a new fault line, told her everything. As if he had only just learned what it was for. Honestly, it was a little flattering.

But then he looked at her. And his gaze wasn't lost. Wasn't desperate. It was settled. Reached. Like whatever had been vibrating inside him had gone still. Like all the static had cleared. No more tension. No more deflection. Just... James. Quiet, steady, and whole. It was the kind of look that made it impossible to regret a single second of what they'd just done.

She bit the inside of her cheek, trying not to smile. Too late. Because suddenly the image was back. That dumb ant and that dumb string.

To keep James from getting fucked... she fucked him. And somehow, the space between two impossible points had collapsed.

He smiled softly at her. "What."

She closed her eyes. "You were right."

He chuckled. "About what?"

"A Wrinkle in Time."

JAMES

She said it like a joke. But it wasn't one. <u>A Wrinkle in Time</u>. It landed between them like truth. Or grace. Or both.

And he couldn't say anything. Not really. He just looked at her. Still trying to understand how she'd done it. Folded space. Closed the distance. Reached him.

How they'd crossed from paper to skin. From Westwood to Lompoc. From two imagined voices to two real bodies, making a real mess. From the con to this colossal reality.

Then the buzz came. Harsh. Mechanical. Final.

He flinched slightly at the sound. She didn't.

She stood first, smoothing her dress, adjusting nothing, looking perfect. He stood a beat later. Still rebooting.

And then, without a word, she stepped in. Arms around his neck. Eyes steady.

And kissed him. Soft and certain. Final.

Just gratitude. Just *yes*. A kiss that said: *Even if this is all we get, it was worth it.*

He let himself close his eyes. Let himself feel it. Let himself stop running. It wasn't the kiss that undid him. It was the kiss that put him back together.

And then–still close, still breathing her in–he whispered into her mouth. Softly, like a vow he knew he couldn't break. "I'll write, I promise."

Nashville/Lompoc - 2012

40.

Dear James,

I don't know where you are. I don't even know if this will reach you. I'm sending it to Lompoc, but you're not there anymore. Still, I wanted to write. Maybe for you. Maybe for me.

It's almost Christmas. I thought I'd feel lonely. But I mostly feel tired.

Because I'm pregnant.

I said it out loud to my bathroom mirror first, just to test it. Then I whispered it to the rats in the lab. Then I sat on the floor with two test sticks in my hand and tried to imagine you reading this.

And, perhaps it goes without saying, perhaps it's more for me than you, but I'm keeping it.

Not because I'm brave. Not because I have a plan. But because I can't imagine giving this child away. Because I can't imagine walking away from someone so fully there. Because I want this child to enter a world excitedly waiting for her.

This kid. She's yours. Mine. Ours.

By the way, it's a girl.

I don't know if I'll raise her alone. I don't know if you'll ever read this. I don't even know if I'll hear from you again.

But I wanted you to know.

Merry Christmas.

Yours,

Minjee

P.S. I still consider you my boyfriend.

Seoul/Nashville - 2013

41.

Dear Minjee,

Merry Christmas and Happy New Year!

I'm alive. And relatively free. Not in prison. Not in transit. Not in legal purgatory.

I now live in a tiny apartment in Seoul. Okay, "apartment" is too generous. It's more like a closet. With its own toilet. It's called a goshiwon and ironically, it's only slightly smaller than my prison cell.

I'm working too, sort of. My mom's youngest sister's husband's brother's kid's business. A moving company for these giant high-rises in Korea. They move totally differently here. It's a whole thing.

I'll explain everything soon, I promise. I'll write you a real letter. Not just this dashed-off stream-of-consciousness shit. I'm no James Joyce.

But I wanted to write to you as soon as I could. That is, if you still want to write. If you're still talking to me. If you haven't (reasonably) moved on. If you've sent me a Dear James letter and I just haven't gotten it yet... that's okay. To-

tally fine. I'll be fine. I want to wish you well. Just let me know and I'll back-date the breakup.

But on the off chance that we're still boyfriend-girlfriend, I have so much to tell you. So much to ask.

Also, I made songpyun for New Year's! I can't wait to tell you more about it. I'm sure we'll turn it into a double entendre somehow.

Yours,
James

Noryangjin Neighborhood, Seoul - February 20, 2013

James was building a spreadsheet. Nothing sketchy. Nothing encrypted. Just... columns. Formulas. Notes in the margins. A little draft called: FOREIGN_CLIENT_STRATEGY.xlsx

Because it had hit him earlier that day, watching an American expat marvel at a plastic wrapped cube of tables, dining chairs, a couch, boxes of clothes, and kitchen supplies swing twenty stories up the side of a building. Foreigners had no idea how this worked.

Foreigners thought moving meant sweating through stairwells, cramming couches into narrow elevators, carrying boxes in human chains. They didn't know about the cranes. They didn't know about the ladder trucks. They didn't know you could take out a sliding glass panel from the veranda and slide an entire apartment's worth of furniture in through the air.

It was big machines. Weights and angles. Logistics.

And apparently, having a Korean-American ex-felon on staff who could speak flawless English and actually think in systems helped.

He'd felt it today. That thing he used to feel. The *click*. The alignment of needs and assets and untapped markets.

And now he was crouched over his tiny table, in his even tinier goshiwon, fingers flying across the keyboard, a half-eaten Shin Ramyeon steaming beside him.

It was almost eleven.

He rolled up the sleeves on his thin white thermal and wiped away a red splash of soup from his gray sweatpants. Comfortable. Focused. A little hyped from the sodium.

He didn't hear the knock at first. Because no one ever knocked on his door. No one even knew he was here.

It came again. Soft but certain.

He paused, one hand hovering above the trackpad, eyes flicking toward the door.

Maybe someone was lost. There were a lot of college students in the building.

He stood up, walked barefoot across the laminate floor, and opened the door.

At first, he only saw a white hood. Framing her face like a halo. Puffy. Ridiculous. Like something conjured out of the cold or a dream.

She wasn't looking at him. She was looking off to the side, like she was still gathering herself. Like maybe she wasn't even sure this was the right door.

That inky hair, flipped out. Just like Minjee's.

And then she turned. Eyes lighter than he remembered. Lashes dark and curled. Full lips. So impossibly pink. All framed in white.

And for a second, he genuinely wasn't sure if he was awake. He didn't know if this was her or someone who looked like her. Or maybe just the idea of her, made real. The kind of impossible moment Gatsby chased. One where she'd come to him.

She turned from the hard-shell carry-on, a backpack perched precariously on top. Her white puffy jacket fell open. Soft black travel clothes. Yoga pants. And a form-fitting shirt stretched gently over her belly.

Pregnant.

Yonsei Hospital, Seoul - June 4, 2013

Minjee was asleep. Her hair still a little damp from exertion. From exhaustion. With one hand, he tucked a strand behind her ear. Smoothed her bangs to the side.

Her parents had left just a moment ago. Quiet goodbyes and empty coffee cups. Their murmured English fading with the sound of elevators closing. They were staying nearby, in a hotel she'd picked herself.

They weren't thrilled about the pregnancy. They were definitely not thrilled about him. But the moment they saw Dohee, she won them over.

James sat in the chair beside the bed, holding her. Wrapped in a cotton hospital blanket. All squint and breath and new skin. Didn't smell like kumquats. Not yet.

Dohee. Do, path. *Hee,* splendid.

The kind of name that carried its own weight. Had its own glow. He felt it like a quiet story. That the long, hard, improbable road they walked had led somewhere real. That their story didn't just survive. It outlasted. *It inspired.*

He whispered it to her. Over and over. "You're wanted, you're wanted." Softly. Like a prayer. Like a vow. Not just to her. To the baby Minjee once was. To the boy he used to be. To all the versions of themselves that had been too much or not enough. To all the people they'd been, in all the lives they lived. To every story that said they weren't allowed to have this. To want this.

"You're wanted."

Acknowledgments

Thank you to MBVR for telling me this story. For any curious readers: *yes, it was real.* The craziest, most unbelievable parts? Those were the true ones.

> *A Korean-American adoptee at UCLA was randomly matched to a Korean pen pal in prison. They exchanged letters for about six months. She visited. She got pregnant. He got deported. They now have an older daughter and a younger son and, at least from the family photo I saw, appear to be living in their "happily ever after."*

That's it. That's all I know. Everything else is made up.

Thank you to those two people. Truly.

Thank you to the friends who read early drafts of Part 1, banged out between 8:30 p.m. (kid bedtime) and 4:30 a.m. one night, then run through ChatGPT (my editor extraordinaire) the next. Originally, this was supposed to be a few notes. A project for the post-career phase of my life, after I've revolutionized data science education, R&D in edtech, higher ed systems, and maybe throw in housing policy in Los Angeles, while also being a mom and a wife.

But my highly biased friends told me Part 1 felt like a real book. They demanded Part 2. (Looking at you MBVR, SM, Blumey, Erin, Tiffany, Emily, Audrey, Laura, Janet, LaTeira,

Betsy, Erica, Patricia, Lizi, Cathy, and Jen!) So I kept writing. Kept wondering: *how did they get together?*

And so, the rest was born. In late nights. In airports. On Saturdays in the office when I was definitely supposed to be working on an NSF proposal.

Thank you to a number of crucial people:

To Sergio, my prison consultant and pastor friend. Thank you for buying me coffee in a sunny Boyle Heights café and walking me through hand jobs, blow jobs, and vaginal intercourse in state and federal prison visitation rooms. And thank you to our long-suffering spouses for giving us full permission to have that extraordinarily explicit, deeply strange, and highly useful conversation between a pastor and another pastor's wife.

To SM, my federal prison visitation consultant. I'm sure the liberties I took were horrifying, but hopefully entertaining enough to be forgiven.

To Jenny Chow, who helped me realize I should buy my own ISBNs.

And to JWS, for tolerating every single goddamn "so" in this manuscript. This book will never be as important as our stats textbook, but thanks for reading it anyway.

Thank you to all my wonderful friends who have let me into your lives through your banter, your obsessions, and your heartbreaks. You are all in here, woven into Minjee and James.

Thank you to two authors I've never met: To Abby Jimenez, for writing Just for the Summer, the book that kickstarted my rom-com reading binge. And to Katherine

Center, who once said that romance novels don't need spoiler alerts. We already know they end up together. That's not the point. The point is anticipation. So even if we already know how the real thing ends, there's still joy in reading (and writing!) the story of how they might have got there.

Finally, thank you to Nathan, Amos, and Dave. You not only listened to me prattle on about rom-coms and <u>The Long Con</u>, but Dave, you donated your fondness for Gatsby. Amos, you lent me your unshakable belief that I could actually write a novel. And Nathan, you trained me your whole life by demanding compelling, narratively creative stories (with "question game"). You gave me honest, often brutal feedback until I shaped up. All your love–and the love I've been so generously given by my friends, community, and God–is the reason I can write a love story at all. Thank you.

About the Author

Ji Y. Son has a PhD in cognitive science and is a fully tenured professor at Cal State LA. None of that helped her write this novel. She usually writes to secure million-dollar research grants aimed at improving STEM education at scale. Or to co-author statistics textbooks. Those skills were also not deployed here.

She does tell jokes in her 8 a.m. stats class and once declared to Ali Wong that she's the "Ali Wong of data science education." That may be the most relevant academic experience for this book, her first romance novel.

She lives in Los Angeles with her husband, two adorable sons, and one tortoise that will outlive them all. Her favorite social network is LinkedIn. Obviously. linkedin.com/in/jiyunson

ALTERNATIVE BOOK COVER

THE
LONG CON

J. Y. SON

A FICTIONAL TRIBUTE
TO SOMETHING IMPOSSIBLY TRUE.